# The Boss Man's Daughter 2

# Lock Down Publications & Ca$h Presents
# *The Boss Man's Daughter 2*

.

## Lock Down Publications

P.O. Box 1482
Pine Lake, Ga 30072-1482

Visit our website at **www.lockdownpublications.com**

First Edition April 2017
Printed in the United States of America
*This is a work of fiction. Names, characters, places, and incidents either are products of the author's imagination or are used fictitiously. Any similarity to actual events or locales or persons, living or dead, is entirely coincidental.*

**Cover design and layout by:** Dynasty's Cover Me
**Book interior design by**: Shawn Walker
**Edited by:** Mia Rucker

# Stay Connected with Us!

Text **LOCKDOWN** to 22828 to stay up-to-date with new releases, sneak peaks, contests and more…

Thank you!

# Submission Guideline.

Submit the first three chapters of your completed manuscript to ldpsubmissions@gmail.com, subject line: Your book's title. The manuscript must be in a .doc file and sent as an attachment. Document should be in Times New Roman, double spaced and in size 12 font. Also, provide your synopsis and full contact information. If sending multiple submissions, they must each be in a separate email.

Have a story but no way to send it electronically? You can still submit to LDP/Ca$h Presents. Send in the first three chapters, written or typed, of your completed manuscript to:

LDP: Submissions Dept

Po Box 1482

Pine Lake, Ga 30072

*DO NOT send original manuscript. Must be a duplicate.*

Provide your synopsis and a cover letter containing your full contact information.

Thanks for considering LDP and Ca$h Presents.

# Acknowledgements

All the glory to God for the gifts he continues to bless me with. I'm forever grateful. I have to thank the love of my life and best friend for continuing to support me, even when I'm an asshole. I don't have the words to tell you what you mean to me, but hopefully you know. I have to thank my Grumpy Bear and my Kiddoodle for inspiring me and loving me. I have to thank my family, and I don't use that word loosely, so if I don't fuck with you, don't think that I do. I most definitely have to thank my loyal fans and readers because you keep me in the lab trying to create the next masterpiece for you. #Nodayzoff! I have to thank my LDP fam for the continued love and support everybody gives me. It's real and I sincerely appreciate that. I have to thank Coffee one time because those new edits are kicking my ass, but I'ma show you what this pen do. LOL! I have to thank Cash for knowing when to say no, especially when I ain't trying to hear that shit. One day I'ma be like you. So know that I'm studying. As always, I have to thank my haters and critics for being so beautiful and talented at what they do. Wait, what is it you do again? LOL! You ain't busy enough BITCH!!! If you get your life you can miss mine a little less. I'm just saying…and to anyone I forgot I'ma be real and tell you that it might not have been an accident. You mad, or nah? We both know you ain't gonna do nothing about it. LOL!!

# Dedication

This book is dedicated to the father and step-father I lost. Wherever you are, I hope I've made you proud.

Aryanna

# Chapter 1
## Fathergod

"I want you inside of me."

"And I want you to stop talking and put my dick back in your mouth," I replied, releasing a cloud of weed smoke in the air.

I could see the briefest hint of attitude flash in her dark brown eyes, but she was smart enough to do as she was told. Maybe, if she hadn't spoken out of turn, I would've willingly given her what she asked for because I'd been eyeing her tight little chocolate figure all week. She had the slim build and athletic grace of a dancer with just the right amount of curves for a nigga to hold on to. Plus, she was cute in the face. Her only flaw was that if she were light skinned, she'd look too much like my baby mama.

It had been years since I saw Sapphire's face in my mind. But in the last few weeks, her image seemed to live with me, almost like it was taunting me. I hadn't wished death on her that fateful night, despite the fact that she was fucking with the enemy and had brought him to my doorstep with murderous intentions. In hindsight, I'd often wished things could've gone down another way, but one of the first things you learn in prison is that wishing is for suckas who didn't wanna survive. It didn't matter that I'd been given a life sentence I still had to survive for my daughters, and so the regrets and everything that came with them had to be buried.

In silence, I'd lived with the pain my decisions had forced on my little girls as I watched them find their way from a distance. For years I'd lived on edge, always wondering if the day would ever come that they finally spoke about the hate they must've felt for me because I'd robbed them of two parents. But it never came. I got their love and support instead, and at times, that made me feel worse. But now that I knew the truth, I was more thankful than ever for the bond we had. To say I was anything other than homicidal in terms of anger would've been an understatement.

To find out that Sapphire was alive, that she'd not only betrayed me, but our children as well, had my thoughts on a steady diet of murder and mayhem. So, as much as I wanted to bless the chick kneeling before me with the dick I knew I shouldn't, truthfully, the only reason she'd been giving me head for the last hour was because I considered her to be on her knees praying to Fathergod. In the end, she would learn that I wasn't merciful. Taking another toke from the blunt of Banna Kush in my hand, I watched her head bob rhythmically up and down, feeling myself trying to knock her vocal cords loose every time she took more than half of me down her throat. I had to admire her determination because it wasn't her lack of skill that wouldn't allow me to cum. It was her resemblance to Sapphire. A knock on the bedroom door startled me and her, but I put my hand on the back of her head to keep her focused on the task at hand.

"What is it?" I called out.

"Kamile just called and said she was on her way."

"A'ight," I replied, knowing that I was gonna have to finish this situation up.

"Stand up and take your clothes off," I said, pushing her away from me, and putting my blunt in the ashtray next to the bed.

She rose to her full 5'6" height and quickly shimmed out of the black miniskirt and white halter top she had on. I wasn't surprised to see that she had nothing on underneath or how good she looked naked. It was just a shame all that had to go to waste.

"Come here," I demanded, laying back on the bed so she could climb on top of me.

Whatever restrictions her mouth had didn't exist with her pussy because she got on top of me and took all I had to offer without blinking. She was tight and wet, though, so I had no complaints.

"This pussy good ain't it?" she asked, riding me slow and steady.

"Stop talking and fuck," I replied, grabbing her hips and lifting up into her.

I got no arguments, and the fact that she was taking dick like a champ kinda turned me on. I watched in fascination as her eyes continued to fill with lust and hunger, seeing the woman moving above me now, but also seeing Sapphire from years ago.

"Ugh. Ugh. Fa-Fathergod," she moaned, riding faster, chasing that light at the end of the tunnel.

I kept pace with her while letting her maintain control. But once she came, I knew the time had come. Quickly, I flipped her on her back, and began delivering those pounding strokes that I knew would make her eyes roll blissfully to the back of her skull.

I felt her legs wrap around me as she pulled me in closer, but only I knew that was a mistake. When I first put my hands around her neck, I only applied enough pressure to give that erotic sensation, and within a few more strokes, she was cumming again. Slowly, I squeezed a little harder until her eyes no longer rolled in ecstasy, but were now staring into mine with slight concern.

My right hand supported my weight as I continued hammering her with blows that had her pussy gushing, and my left hand continued tightening around her throat. It's a thrilling thing to watch panic and passion fight inside a person, because even though I was now choking her in a way that made it hard to breathe, there was still blatant hunger for sexual satisfaction in her eyes.

"This dick is good, ain't it?" I whispered into her ear.

Her response was inaudible, which surprised no one except her. When her legs unwrapped from my waist I knew the beginnings of fear were taking hold of her, and that made me enjoy the longer strokes I was giving her.

I could tell I'd found her g-spot because the eye rolling was involuntary and her pussy was spasming like a major eruption was coming. My own climax was within reach, but I needed her to get there, which made me squeeze a little harder. When her eyes focused in on mine, the hunger was gone and all that remained was raw, unbridled fear.

"There's my Sapphire," I said.

Her hands went to the one I had around her throat, but she was clawing in vain because my grip wouldn't loosen until I was ready. Despite the chocolate hue on her complexion I noticed her face changing colors. There was no more fear in her eyes, though, it was outright terror, and that was just the way I wanted it.

"Please," she croaked, but it was too late.

Tightening my grip for the last time, I completely shut off her air supply and watched the light dim in her eyes while her body bucked beneath me. My vision swam as I came hard, but I still got to see her struggle for her last breath that wouldn't reach her lungs in time. I climbed off of her feeling somewhat better, although I knew this was only a temporary fix until I got my hands on the real Sapphire.

"Fathergod, you got a visitor," came a voice from outside the bedroom door.

Grabbing the white halter top off the floor, I wiped my dick off before tucking myself back inside my jeans, and going to my dresser drawer for a t-shirt.

Once I was presentable, I walked out into the living room where I found Kamile sitting on the white leather couch drinking a smoothie.

"Ms. Armstrong, how are you?" I asked, sitting in the matching loveseat across from her.

"Better than you, Johnathan,"

"You know damn well that ain't true, and you're not old enough to use my first name," I said, motioning for one of my associates sitting at the kitchen table to roll me a blunt.

"The fact that I'm 24 years old doesn't change the fact that I'm a boss, which puts us on an even playing field, Johnathan. And despite your net worth, I'm definitely doing better than you because my name and face ain't on every news station or at the top of every agency's wanted list."

"What's your point, Kamile?"

"My point is that I don't think it's a good idea for you to be here. Plus, I hate lying to Free."

I could tell by the way she looked away when she said my daughter's name that this was what had her more concerned than the feds. After I'd explained to Freedom and Destiny that the reason the feds had made me disappear was because I'd found out about Sapphire being alive, I'd convinced them not to go on the run.

There was no proof they'd kidnapped the senator's son to get me out, and Angel needed them by her side while she was locked up because I couldn't be there. The trade-off was that I'd had to agree to leave the country and go to Moscow so the feds couldn't bring me back. I'd agreed and gotten on the plane, but I'd made a detour to Chicago and had Kamile lie for me since she owned a few strip clubs in Russia.

I couldn't leave my girls at a time like this. Plus, the only way I'd found out about Sapphire was because the Black Guerilla Family was looking at a RICO case and she'd helped them build it. Not only had the bitch destroyed my life and our kids' lives, but now she was coming for the family that had been down for me since day one. A real nigga couldn't run away and let her live after all of that.

"You ain't gotta be worried about Free, Kamile, she ain't gonna find out I'm in Chicago," I said, taking the lit blunt offered to me.

"With all due respect, you been gone a long time and your daughter has a long reach. If she does find out that you're up here, or the feds get you, it's my ass she's coming for."

I wouldn't insult her intelligence by discussing this as something that couldn't happen, because I knew how Free got down. I just had to make sure it didn't come to that.

"I'll worry about Free. Have you heard anything about Sapphire?" I asked.

"Nah, but between my channels and yours we'll find out where she's at. My guess is the feds are keeping her location top secret, especially with you now loose to do only God knows what."

"Up the ante then. I got five million for whoever can get her in front of me," I said, passing her the blunt.

"Five mil, huh?"

"Yep, I want her nothing ass that bad for everything she's done."

"I'll get on top of it immediately," she replied, hitting the blunt twice before passing it back.

"You heard anything about Angel?"

"It's only been a week, Johnathan, but Free did say that there's a bond hearing coming up. They're trying to stay positive, but she was just involved in a similar situation only weeks ago," she replied.

"Fuck that. I need to go down there and get my baby out," I said, standing up.

"Sit down, Johnathan."

For a second I was taken aback at her forceful tone of voice, but it made me really study the young woman before me. She was beautiful, standing at 5'5" and weighing maybe a light one hundred forty pounds. Even with the hazel eyes and kissable honey complexion, it was clear she was more than just a gorgeous face and a nice body, and I was curious as to what she was about. So, I sat down.

"You know as well as I do that an irrational and emotional move like going to Tennessee ain't how you do shit. I don't know you to kick it with, but I know your legacy, and that ain't how Fathergod would rock. I know that's your child, but you prepared all of them to play any position necessary to survive, so trust them."

Knowing she was right didn't make it any easier to sit by and let this shit play out, but it was what I had to do. I wouldn't be sitting idle, though. I was definitely gonna make some shit happen because a lot of people thought I was gone for good. A surprise was coming.

"You're right, Ms. Armstrong, and I'ma play my position. What you gonna do, though?"

"I'ma do the same because my position is one of the most important ones," she replied, standing up and smoothing the wrinkles out of the black blazer she was rocking over her matching body suit.

It was a struggle to keep my eyes on her face and not on her curves.

"And what's your position?" I asked.

"Everyone knows I'm the right hand of God," she replied, smiling mischievously and heading for the front door.

"We'll see," I said before the door closed and she disappeared from view.

There was no doubt she was interesting, but the question was whether she'd be an asset or a liability. I had no room for the latter.

"Call somebody up here to get that bitch's body out my bedroom," I ordered the young soldier sitting at the table.

I didn't even know her name, but I knew her death was just one of many. I wasn't playing for trophies, I was playing for keeps.

# Chapter 2
## Angel

"So, how good are my chances at getting bail?"

"Come on, Angel, I just got you a sweetheart deal for the last two people you killed, so you know how bad this looks. You're a convicted felon so you're not even supposed to be near a gun," she replied, clearly frustrated.

"Miranda, you're the best lawyer money can buy, and I know my sister just dropped half a million on you this morning. You need to earn it."

"Angel, you know I'm gonna do everything I can for you. I mean everyone who was working the night shift, plus the few customers that were there, gave consistent statements about what happened. You were once again defending Devontae, even the camera footage shows that. The problem is that the slugs they pulled out of one of the victims match an earlier massacre that took place in a strip club. They found the gun, and it don't have any prints on it, but it's either yours or Vontae's. If you tell them he-"

"I ain't telling them shit, and if you suggest that again, I'ma put my hands on you," I warned her, stopping my pacing back and forth in front of the desk that separated us in the attorney/client room.

I knew how bad shit looked. I mean it was all over the fucking news, but I wasn't about to snitch on King Deuce or implicate him in any way. That wasn't how the game went.

"Listen, I know you live by the code of the streets and I respect that, but I wouldn't be a good lawyer if I didn't tell you exactly how bad this looks. First of all, you two were just involved in a shooting a couple weeks ago. To a jury, that either looks like you've got the weirdest luck in the world or you're a part of this Hoover Crip gang situation. It doesn't help that the two dudes you and Vontae shot are certified gang members, also Hoover Crips. You've got a gunshot wound that's no more than a week old, and they took a blood sample, which I'm guessing will at some point tie you to the strip club. And let us not forget that you're on probation with a suspended sentence over your head. The body count in the club was twenty-four people, some unsavory characters, but others were working girls of the establishment. Bottom line is that we're talking the death penalty on a guilty verdict," she said sincerely.

I'd always known there was a high probability that it could come down to that, but to actually have those words spoken was like getting a gut punch while I was on my period. Could they be real about putting a 22-year-old on death row? The list of shit she'd just run down to me had crossed my mind a million different ways in the last week I'd spent in the Criminal Justice Center in Nashville, Tennessee. So, I knew it all added up to being the worst kind of bad, but that still didn't mean I could roll on my brother KD. There had to be another way.

"I ain't cooperating, so you need to find another way," I said, resuming my slow pacing back and forth in the tiny room.

I could read the frustration in Miranda's demeanor, but I knew she could see the determination in mine.

I may not have had the pampering I was used to, and I was rocking some straight back cornrows, but I was by no means a broken woman. I was the daughter of Fathergod himself, and that meant I was built to last.

"When is my bail hearing?" I asked.

"It's scheduled for 9am tomorrow."

"Will my sisters be there?"

"I'm not sure. They've been trying to keep a low profile because they're under round the clock FBI surveillance, and I've advised them to maintain their distance for now," she replied, hesitantly.

"Why would you do that?" I asked, stopping in front of her once again.

"Because as far your name and your father's name ain't came up in the same sentence publicly, and I wanna keep it that way as long as possible. Despite your sister's alibis, the feds are on them tough, but for right now it looks like you've been busy doing your own thing. You gotta remember that the jury pool is gonna be from somewhere in this state, and the minute you're linked to a legendary gangsta like Johnathan "Fathergod" Walker, you won't get a fair trial in fifty states."

I knew she was right, and she was just trying to keep shit real with me because there was no need to sell illusions. That didn't stop the physical ache I was feeling to be near my sisters, or just to see their faces in the crowd to know they were there with me. I didn't doubt their love or loyalty in any way. We'd just never allowed anything to separate us until this.

"So, aside from the KD angle, what's our best defense?" I asked, sitting in the fold out chair across from her.

"Well... I could argue self-defense for the whole Burger King fiasco, but honestly they're more focused on the twenty-four people killed in that strip club. After that situation that happened in that Orlando night club last year, this situation is gonna be viewed as an act of terrorism."

"What do you mean?" I asked, feeling nauseous as my stomach dropped.

"What I mean is that at some point the feds are gonna come talk to you, and they may or may not offer you a deal."

"I'm not-"

"Yeah, I know, you're not snitching. The hard truth is that one of you is going down for what happened in that club. Let's hope that Vontae is as loyal to you as you are to him," she said, closing her briefcase and standing up.

I didn't have any doubts about who King Deuce was or what he stood for, but that still didn't help me to figure out how the fuck I could get out of this mess.

"I'll see you in the morning," she said, banging on the door so the officer would open it and let her out.

I didn't want her to leave because I still had so many questions, but I knew she didn't have the answers I wanted. There was no magical fix to this situation, not even with all the power that came with my family. Still, there was no way to accept that I would die in this place or behind bars in any institution. I couldn't go out like that.

"Hands behind your back, Walker," the cop ordered, once he'd let Miranda out.

I did as I was instructed, knowing I'd never get used to the feel or sound of handcuffs on my wrists.

Some of the dancers I knew used to tell stories about wild nights they'd had with both men and women involving handcuffs, but there was no way that shit would ever be sexy to me. Most bitches didn't have to be cuffed everywhere they went, but apparently, I was special and somewhat famous, making me a part of an exclusive club in here.

After I was cuffed and groped, or what they call being patted down, I was led from the room and back downstairs to the dungeon. I didn't get to live and mingle with general population. Instead I was housed on a floor one level below the main floor with the rest of the real killers. I had no idea if KD was experiencing the same shit on his side of the jail, but it was definitely that serious on my end.

There were ten units on this floor and each of them held five cells a piece, with one inmate per sell. The upside was that I didn't have to smell another bitch's funky pussy every time she had to piss. Plus I didn't have to share my food. It did get boring day in and day out sitting in a cell by myself because it was evident from the jump that these bitches didn't like out of towner's.

"What's up with my lunch?" I asked, once we'd arrived at the front door to my unit.

"Why you worried 'bout a brown bag with some sandwiches when you got a cell full of commissary, big money?"

"Because it's my bag lunch, so can I get it?"

"Yeah, well, I put them all on the table. See if you can find it," he replied sarcastically, taking the handcuffs off and pushing me through the door.

The units were small, and when you walked in the shower was to the immediately left, not a foot from the door. The five cells were on the right, there was a metal table built into the wall in the back, and there was a phone positioned in the middle of the wall on the left. I'd seen shoe boxes that were bigger, and when you put angry bitches in close quarters like this, you could guarantee drama.

As I heard the door close behind me, I could see what type of day this was gonna be, but the cop had made it unavoidable. The cute little Puerto Rican chick named Rose was on the phone with her back to everyone else, most likely crying with one of her four kids on the phone. I could hear the shower running, and the sounds of passion coming from behind the curtain which meant the two white girls, Cassidy and Gisle, were doing what they do. And in the back of the unit, Renata was sitting at the table acting like she was reading a book.

I didn't see my bag lunch, and if anybody ate it, my money was on the big bitch. She was about 6'3", weighing at least two hundred pounds, and she thought she was a bully. So far, we'd avoided colliding, but I knew the day would come because she felt like I had to be tested. There could only be one light-skin queen running shit, and I knew her ugly ass felt like I was too pretty for the job. It was time to show her she was wrong.

"Where's my bag lunch, Renata?" I asked, walking up to the table.

Her response was to lick her index finger and turn the page of the book she was reading by some author named Asad, completely ignoring me and my question. In a situation like this, my dad had taught us the rules of engagement clearly. The book she was holding in front of her face didn't allow her to see my left hook coming, but she damn sure felt it when I connected. Her nose gushed blood instantly, but I didn't care because I was already sending a follow up right jab to the same location.

"Bitch," she exclaimed, trying to stand up and defend herself. But I was already on her ass with what little hair she had wrapped in my left hand while I swung my right in fierce determination.

This was probably the point where I was supposed to talk to her while beating that ass so she understood where she fucked up, but I wasn't about to waste my breath. Every time she opened her mouth to speak, I tried to shove my fist down her throat. It only took two teeth scattering across the floor before she decided to keep her mouth closed. Then she was trying to ball up and protect her face. So I dragged her to the floor, delivering two swift kicks to her body with my jail issued Chuck Taylors before backing away.

"Next time you eat my shit, bitch, I'ma cut you," I warned, continuing to back up towards my cell door as two cops rushed in the front door.

"Lock down, Walker," they ordered, shoving me in my cell and slamming the door in my face.

It felt good to relieve some of the stress I'd been feeling ever since the night I was arrested. I knew it wouldn't do me any favors when it came time for my bail hearing tomorrow, but I couldn't sacrifice my respect if I expected to survive in here.

I watched as the two cops picked Renata up off the floor, admiring the blood still pouring from her nose and mouth, and her quickly swelling left eye. I knew they'd keep me locked in my room until I went to court tomorrow, but I didn't give a fuck. After washing my hands, I sat down at the small table next to my bed, picking up the cheap ass security pen the jail issued and a piece of paper. It was looking like I'd be here for a while and so it was time to learn all I could about this jungle. And I knew just the lion to teach me.

# Chapter 3
### Freedom

"I wanna see you."

"You know I wanna see you too, but we can't do that right now," I replied softly.

"It's 2 in the morning, Free, I can sneak in and-"

"Baby, listen. You know I'm not used to being without you by my side, but this is bigger than us right now. We hotter than fish grease. All eyes are on us, and I can't have you under the same scrutiny or the money will dry up. Now ain't the time for that to happen."

I hadn't expected him to keep trying to convince me to let him come over, but his loud silence let me know that he wanted to do just that. Bone and I had been inseparable for years, so much so that it was strange for both of us right now, but it was necessary.

The feds were on me and Destiny like flies on shit, trying to see if we'd lead them to our father. So, we had to move cautiously. That meant only phone contact between us and the streets, not even Big Baby and Lil Boy were allowed at Angel's condo, where we'd been hiding out. We needed our wolves out there to hunt when necessary and that meant sacrifices had to be made.

"How is everything?" I asked, changing the subject.

"You know shit is running like clockwork, but we are running low."

That wasn't something I wanted to hear, considering my connect was locked up with my sister, but 50 keys of good dope only went so far, no matter how much you stepped on it. A drought was the last thing I needed because between paying for Angel's defense and supporting my father while he was on the run, we were gonna blow through money.

"I've got a plan I'm working on. How long do you think we have?" I asked.

"Maybe a couple weeks, but you know I hate to push it."

"A'ight, I'm on it. I'll call you later to check in."

"How are you feeling? Have you been sleeping?" he asked.

I could hear the worry in his voice and I knew, no matter what I said, it wouldn't go away. That wasn't a bad thing, though.

"Baby, I'm fine. I promise. I sleep as much as I need to, and I feel fine, except for the cabin fever starting to set in."

"Well you can always come out and visit me," he suggested slyly.

"Bone."

"Okay, I'll stop pushing. Try to get some rest and I'll talk to you in a few hours."

"I will. I love you."

"Love you, too, baby," he replied, hanging up.

What I'd really wanted to say was come over and be with me, hold me. I wanted that comfort only he could give because it was only moments such as these where I could actually admit how ugly shit was.

I was prepared to pay whatever to secure Angel's freedom, but Miranda had kept it real with me by telling me that there might not be enough money in the world.

I couldn't put words to the guilt I felt. I was so focused on getting my father back that I'd allowed my sister to put herself in harm's way. If I didn't have such a one-track mind, I would've told both her and King Deuce that that whole situation could've waited. Now I was without my father and my sister. Plus, I couldn't make the moves needed to fix this shit.

"Still can't sleep, huh?" Destiny asked, walking into the kitchen.

Even from the spot on the couch and the dim lights, I could see the bags under her eyes.

"Nah. It don't look like you been to sleep either."

"I keep thinking about Angel. I mean, if it was me or you in there, I could understand because we do what we do out here. But her luck is just bad, for real."

"You ain't never lied. We gotta figure out a way to get her ass out of there," I said, wondering what she was doing at this very moment.

"Well, we know it ain't gonna happen the legal way, so what's the plan?"

"To be honest, I can't even think straight," I replied, laying down on the couch and staring at the ceiling.

"All that stress ain't good for you… or the baby."

The baby. Somehow in the complete chaos that was my life in the last week since we'd gotten our dad back and lost him again, and Angel got locked up, I'd found the time to take a pregnancy test. I couldn't deny it anymore, although my mind hadn't exactly accepted the idea of me being a mom. On more than one occasion, I'd mentally ran through the pros and cons of having an abortion.

It wasn't that I was against having kids, but now damn sure didn't seem like the time or place to invite them into the world. Knowing this had me asking myself if it was better to have an abortion or a miscarriage. Of course, I couldn't talk to Bone about any of this because whether it was planned or not, he'd made it clear that he wanted me to have his baby.

"There's no way I can't be stressed, but I'm doing the best I can."

"Good because I can't wait to be an auntie," she said, bringing me a glass of orange juice and sitting it on the table.

"Yeah, I bet, until you start getting those phone calls to come get this bad little mufucka before I kill 'em."

"I don't think my niece or nephew is gonna be bad. I mean, from what I experienced, you're a good mom, Free. A hell of a lot better than ours was."

We hadn't really talked about the bomb our dad had dropped on us about our mother still being alive, and working overtime to destroy the organization he'd help build. Truthfully, I didn't even know how to process her not being dead. Every time I tried I got so angry thinking about all the times me and my sisters needed her, or how we'd had to grow up without any physical guidance because of her. Hate wasn't a strong enough word for what I felt for Sapphire.

"How could she do it, Free? I know they had their problems, and dad said he could've treated her better, but how could she just throw us away like that?"

The emotion in her voice made me sit up and pull her onto my lap like I used to when we were younger. I was the only mother she'd had when it counted, and no matter how old she got, I'd still be there when she needed that shoulder to cry on.

"I don't know how she could do it or why she did it, but I'm glad she did," I said sincerely.

"You are?" she asked, looking at me with tears in her eyes that did little to hide how lost she truly felt.

"Yeah, I am, because we wouldn't be who we are if she hadn't left. No matter where dad was, we always had him and he still gave us the love and guidance we needed. So, fuck Sapphire because I don't wanna be anyone except who I am."

I caught a hint of a smile pulling at the corners of her mouth before she took my face in her hands and kissed away the tears I hadn't known were there. Neither of us would cry for the life we had because we both knew the shit could've been worse. The goal now was to figure out how to keep what we had.

"Drink your juice and come on," she said, standing up and passing me the glass.

I did as instructed, and then took her hand when she offered it so she could pull me to my feet.

"Damn, you putting on that baby weight already, ain't you?" she said laughing.

"Fuck you, bitch, I'm still a hundred forty-five pounds, and you know it because you wish you weighed this much."

"I don't need to weigh that much because I'm still as curvy as you are," she replied, pulling me towards Angel's bedroom.

We could pass for twins but I definitely had more curves and this baby on the way would only added to it. I didn't argue, though. I followed her into Angel's room, where we climbed into bed together and talked until sleep finally called us both. Neither of us had been getting the proper amount of sleep for obvious reasons, but actually being together in Angel's bed helped somehow.

I awoke to the smell of sausage cooking, and initially I thought the rumbling in my stomach was hunger until I was forced to bolt from the bed into the bathroom and hug the toilet bowl. I hated morning sickness with a passion, but that didn't lessen the vomit shooting out of my mouth. Finally, after five minutes, all I had left was the dry heaves, and I was able to move from the floor to the sink and rinse my mouth out. I was able to keep a few gulps of water down, and by the time I finished brushing my teeth, I felt halfway normal.

Looking in the mirror prevented me from lying about how run down I really was, though, because I had bags under my eyes darker than Destiny's, and my normal chocolate skin tone looked like it had been in the sun too long. My hazel eyes were mere background colors when compared to the redness surrounding them.

The light streaming through the bathroom window told me it was at least mid-morning, which meant I'd slept a minimum of eight hours. But it was obvious I would need more than that.

What a bitch really needed was a vacation, but that wasn't possible until we got Angel back.

Now that the first wave of morning sickness had passed, the smell of the food had me hungry, so I followed my nose to the kitchen.

"What you are whipping up, chef Baby D?" I asked, sitting down at the table where I could watch my sister work.

Destiny may have been the youngest, and the least domesticated, but the bitch could throw down with the pots and pans.

"I ain't doing much, just some sausage, bacon, eggs, fried potatoes, and homemade cinnamon buns."

"Damn, how long you been up, and what time is it?" I asked, licking my lips in anticipation of the listed menu.

"It's a little after 11am, and I only been up about an hour. I was gonna let you sleep until everything was done, but it should only be another ten minutes anyway."

"Not that I'm complaining or anything, but what made you get up and cook this big breakfast for us?"

"Because we been living off fast food so I just figured we could use something good to eat," she replied, dropping strips of bacon into the pan.

I was definitely tired of ordering take out all the time. We'd eaten at every place within delivering distance, but I could tell by the way she avoided looking at me that there was more to this breakfast. I didn't press it, though. Instead I got up and grabbed my phone off the living room coffee table so I could take care of some pressing business.

"I already got our new phones out of the safe, so when you're done just destroy it," Destiny said.

Being that we knew we were under constant surveillance, we'd been switching phones every seventy-two hours, sometimes sooner if we got a bad feeling. We knew it would be like this so we'd bought as many burner phones as we could on our way back from Maryland. On top of that, we had someone dressed like a maid sweep the house for listen devices whenever we were out. And thanks to a few well-placed dollars, we had access to every computer in the complex. Even with all that, I still had no illusions about the feds capabilities or the pressure they would apply, which was why I had Black Sam monitoring everything from Florida.

"Did you talk to Samantha?" I asked.

"Nah, but I'ma facetime with her in a little while."

"Facetime? I don't think that's a good idea," I replied slowly.

I always tried to keep shit professional with Black Sam, but she was a bad bitch and that was just what Destiny liked.

"We won't talk business like that, Free. I'm not stupid."

"So, why facetime at all?" I asked.

"Because I'm cooped up in the house with you and I can't get no pussy, and she don't mind playing with hers for me. Any more questions?" she asked, laughing.

"Nah, too much information already. Just make sure you handle business before pleasure."

"Yes, mom," she replied, sticking her tongue out at me.

Ignoring her sarcasm, I took my seat back at the kitchen table and sent Kamile a text about the dinner party I wanted to have. I'd met Kamile about five years back when she was opening a club here in Atlanta, and from the jump, I liked her because I knew she was bout that money. If it wasn't about securing the bag, she wasn't about interested, and that was definitely a mentality me and my sisters could understand.

Her being a former dancer helped her relate to Angel, and since she hustled on the side she was a bitch Destiny and I could fuck with, even though I knew Destiny just wanted to fuck her. We'd done business of all kinds over the years, and she'd earned both my trust and my respect. So it only made sense that I went to her when I needed to make sure my dad was good.

I knew he didn't do cold weather, but he could be living a lot worse than in a Russian strip club filled with pussy rotating from all over the world. The most important thing was that I knew he was safe, and that allowed me to focus on the task at hand.

My text to Kamile this morning about my dinner party was my way of telling her I needed weight. One of her side hustles was a catering company, which made her drops easy, and made sure this conversation wouldn't seem out of the ordinary. She hit me back immediately, asking how many guests and what I wanted the menu to consist of, which meant how many keys and what drug. There was no telling how long KD would be locked up with Angel, and I didn't know his connect well enough to deal straight with them, so it was best to make a power move.

I shot her a text back, letting her know that my event was for two hundred people, and of course, the menu was surf and turf. For most people that meant some type of seafood and steak, but in my world, that was a Heroin and Coke mixture known as Baluchi. It was the absolute truth. It took her five minutes to confirm, and I sent Bone a text to pay her and work out the delivery just as Destiny was sitting my plate in front of me.

"That's a lot of food," I said, accepting the fork from her almost intimidated. Almost.

"You eating for two now, so handle your business," she replied, sitting down with her own plate.

"So, are you gonna tell me what this is really about?" I asked.

"What do you mean?"

"I know you, Destiny, and I know when you're keeping something from me. That's the reason your ass got out of my presence the night Angel got shot, because you knew I would've known something was up."

"Are you ever gonna let that go?" she asked.

"Let it go? Bitch, when this is all over, I'm still gonna whoop your ass for keeping that from me. I suggest you not make it worse," I advised, digging into my food.

"I'm not keeping nothing major from you like that. It's just, well, I talked to Miranda while you were asleep because you know Angel had her bail hearing this morning."

"Okay, and?" I asked.

"No bail… and she's on lockdown because she beat a bitch up yesterday."

Hearing that stopped my fork in mid-air as my eyes snapped towards Destiny's.

"Did somebody hurt Angel?" I asked slowly.

"No, from what Miranda said, Angel whooped this big bitch, but she doesn't know why because our sister ain't talking."

"Yeah. And it don't look good against her either. What else did Miranda say?"

All of a sudden Destiny found her food more interesting or important than answering my question because she began eating with enthusiasm.

"I'm not gonna shoot the messenger, so just tell me what she told you," I said patiently.

"You know she can't really give specifics, but she said it don't look good."

"How bad are we talking?" I asked, as my stomach moved in an unsettling way.

"All she said was bad with a capital B."

I needed more than just vague references and Angel needed to know that we were there no matter what.

"Finish eating because we've got shit to do," I said.

"What are we doing?"

"For starters we're going to see our sister."

"But I thought-"

"Fuck what anybody said, that's our sister in there and she needs us," I said forcefully.

"You're right Free. And I'll drive."

# Chapter 4
## Fathergod

Being a wanted man meant I had to stay in hiding, especially given the fact that I didn't exactly blend with other people because of my size. I'd learned long ago that it didn't matter if you were the loudest person in the room or the most quiet, when you were a big nigga, you'd be noticed either way.

After doing a ten year bid, you'd think I'd be sitting still, even in the small 2-bedroom apartment I was now calling home. But something about knowing that the choice to open a door and walk through it was mine made me antsy. It was that inability to sit still that had me walking inside a gentlemen's club called Rain Drops on the west side of Chicago a little after 3am.

I'd taken the necessary precautions of travelling with a pack of my young wolves, and of course, I was secure with the Ruger P229 tucked into my tailored Black Billionaire suit pants. Still I knew when Kamile got the word that I was in her club, she would worry for a few different reasons.

I had no doubt she had the cops on this side of town paid off, but that luxury tax probably only afforded protection for minor incidents. I was literally one of America's most wanted and there weren't a lot of cops who would overlook that. Plus, there could be some rival gang members in the area. None that meant shit to me, though, because Fathergod would live and die on his terms.

"Spread out and cover the room, and make sure we got eyes on the door," I said to my lieutenant, Motey.

Motey looked the part of a devoted Muslim, slender built with a suit and bow tie on, and glasses that topped of his look of dignified intelligence. Deep down he was a killer who wouldn't hesitate to hop in whoever's ass when instructed, and that's why I kept him closer than an American Express black card. As I took in the room full of leather chairs where men sat and women gave them lap dances, Motey relayed my instructions to our crew.

For it to be so late at night, that place was still jumping, although it was clear that the stage was shut down for the night so patrons could get that one on one vibe they were looking for. I hadn't been to that particular spot in years. When I was there last, it was more of an environment to dance and take a bitch home, or catch a body if a nigga wasn't careful. Now, the décor was elegant and the music was more about setting the mood for the fantasy being sold, then busting a move. I made my way to a corner table in the back where I could watch the door and the crowd, and signaled the waitress over to me.

"What can I get you, sir?"

"I want a bottle of Patron 1800," I replied, pulling a wad of money from my pocket.

"Your money is no good here, sir. I'll bring you your order and the boss will be with you momentarily," she said, giving me a smile before making her way to the bar.

It was evident Kamile kept a close eye on her establishment, but that didn't surprise me based on what Free had told me about her. Despite the shit they got themselves into, I believed my daughters had sound judgement when it came to business and who they conducted it with. So, what had surprised me about Kamile was just the sheer force of nature she seemed to be, especially at her age.

"You really are crazy, huh?" she said, appearing out of the shadows.

"Has your hair always been purple?" I asked, noticing the glow of her highlights in contrast to her naturally black color.

I wasn't complaining, though, because at present it matched the purple cat suit she had on, and the way it molded to her body was a thing of beauty.

"Did you really come here to talk about my hair Johnathan?" she asked, sitting in the chair across the table from me.

"No. I really came because I'm tired of being locked up. I just did ten years, and I can't trade one cage of force for another one of my own making."

"So, let me get you out of the country where you can move around without having to worry about being arrested."

"I'm not worried about it now," I replied, smiling.

"Your arrogance is gonna get you caught up and me killed."

"I wouldn't let that happen, sweetheart, you're safe with Fathergod," I said, pouring both of us a shot from the bottle the waitress had just sat between us.

"I'ma need you not to refer to yourself in third person. That's just too much," she replied, tossing her shot back and quickly pouring another.

"You're funny."

"So, what are you really doing here, Johnathan? I mean, I'm sure you were ready to get out of that tiny apartment, but you could've gone anywhere, so why come to me?" she asked.

"I used to come here back in the day when this was a dance spot, before your time, and I was curious to see what you'd done to the place."

"And?" she asked, tossing back her second shot without blinking.

"It's nice in here. You probably make way more money than its previous owner."

"I do a'ight, but that wasn't what I was asking you, Johnathan."

"What are you asking then Kamile?"

"You probably did come out to visit one of your old spots, but I was wondering if you were gonna admit that you came to find out whether or not you wanted to fuck me, and why," she replied with a straight face.

I wasn't one to be surprised easily, but her directness made me pause for a minute before I laughed genuinely.

"Wow, you've got no filter, huh? And what makes you think that I wanna fuck you?" I asked.

"I don't think, I know you wanna fuck me because most men do. I just don't think you've admitted it to yourself or figured out why yet."

"Who's arrogant now?" I asked, drinking my shot and pouring another one to match the lead she already had on me.

"I'm not speaking from an arrogant standpoint, only an observant one. I saw how you looked at me when I was at your place earlier. I know very few people talk to you the way that I did, but it needed saying and you wouldn't respect me if I bullshitted you or let you walk over me. You raised strong women, so it only makes sense that you would want one by your side."

"Wait, so now we've gone from fucking to you being the queen opposite this king? Sounds like you've got an agenda," I replied, making quick work of my second shot.

"No agenda because I'm a queen regardless, and I rule just fine on my own. I was actually complimenting your intelligence because I know you're smart enough to hold on to a good woman once you find her. I will admit that I'm arrogant about how good my pussy is, though, but I'm incredibly stingy with it."

I could see myself getting ready to probably take this conversation somewhere it didn't need to go because I definitely found this woman interesting, if not a bit dangerous.

"Nothing wrong with being a little stingy, I mean, it's not something you just want to give away," I said, pouring myself another shot.

"You've been gone a while, Johnathan, you might wanna go easy on this 1800," she said, taking the shot from my hand and tossing it back.

"I can handle myself."

"Oh, I have no doubts, and I know you came with a crew of fifteen, but just to be on the safe side, I want you to keep your wits about you."

"I will. How late do you stay open anyway?" I asked, pouring another shot and making it disappear before she could snatch it.

"We're open until 5am, but I can get you a private room in the back if you'd like."

"You'd do that for me?" I asked.

"Is that what you want?"

"You tell me, Kamile, you think you can read my mind and know my intentions so well."

"I do. Sit right here and I'll send someone to get you," she said, standing and moving off into the dimly lit room.

I watched the sway of her hips until she disappeared from view, wondering how everything looked under that cat suit when it was bathed in nothing except the moonlights glow. Dangerous thoughts for sure, but tempting nevertheless.

Motey was posted at the bar and I caught his eye, signaling him to come see me.

"We're secure in here and we've got eyes on the street thanks to the owner," he said, sitting in the chair Kamile had recently vacated.

"What do you mean?"

"She's got cameras up and down the block and behind the building. Trust me, no one can sneak up on this mufucka, and she's got two of our soldiers in a room watching the cameras."

I definitely like Ms. Kamile Armstrong's combination. And she's sexy as hell.

"Which one of you fine gentlemen is escorting me to the VIP room?"

The woman who spoke those words was a breathtaking redbone, wearing a barely there black Victoria Secret's bra and panty set with some fire red five inch heels. She couldn't have been more than 5'2" without the heels. Her eyes were a smoky gray, and her body was thoroughbred thick.

"That would be me," I said, standing up to admire her further.

"Right this way," she replied, taking me by the hand and leading me down a dark hallway away from the main room.

Just looking at her from the front, I could tell that that ass would be juicy. But now that I was behind her, I realized I'd had no idea. Halfway down the hall we came to a door that blended into the wall so good that I wouldn't have known it was there if it hadn't opened.

"This definitely wasn't here the last time I was," I said, following her inside.

"Then it must've been a while, but don't worry because you're in good hands," she said sensually, leading me to the black leather couch against the far wall.

The room wasn't huge, but it was big enough for the couch I was now sitting on and the stripper pole right in front of it. Once the door shut, the pole lit up like a seven foot tall black light, illuminating the room while also revealing no cum stains.

"You want me on the pole or you want me up close and personal?" she asked, seductively.

"Whatever you feel, sweetheart."

I don't know where the music came from, but suddenly classic R. Kelly filled the room as he sang about not seeing nothing wrong with a little bump and grind.

"Just relax, daddy, Sweetpea got you," she whispered into my ear, as she climbed on top of me and began her dance.

If my mind served me correct, I wasn't supposed to touch her, but when she put my hands on her big ole ass. Who was I to object? The way the light danced in her eyes was hypnotizing, but it was hard to keep my eyes off her body as she worked her magic.

"Don't be shy. Touch me anywhere you want," she encouraged, putting her titties in my face.

I had no idea how long she'd been at work tonight, but she smelled like sweet gummy bears, and I wanted to taste her.

"No matter what happens, I need you to act like any normal man would in this situation," she whispered in my ear.

I opened my mouth to ask her what she meant, but she put a finger to my lips while using her other hand to unhook her bra. Her titties popped out and damn near hit me in my face, along with the gold wrapper of a magnum condom. Her left hand went for my zipper while she used her mouth and right hand to open the condom. I was confused about what she'd meant with her last statement, but as she pulled my dick out and rolled the condom down it I had no questions about what she was about to do.

"You have to fuck me, but I want you to listen carefully to what I'm gonna tell you," she said, raising up and pulling her panties to the side as she guided me into her.

My senses were on high alert, but her pussy was so wet and tight that I damn near lost my mind. The pace she set was a slow gallop and she held me close while putting her lips directly on my ear.

"I saw you on the news and I know who you are. Dancing is just my side hustle, my 9-5 is as an office assistant for a prominent surgeon. When I saw your face on the news and they started talking about what you'd been doing time for, I was only halfway paying attention, until they showed the picture of your baby's mama. I've seen that bitch before, and her face was burned up, but she wasn't dead. She had a few reconstructive surgeries and when it was over she looked like a completely different person. When I saw you come in tonight, I told Kamile what I knew and she sent me down here."

Despite the fact that I was balls deep in some good pussy, her words had me more excited. I should've guessed that the feds would go above and beyond to protect Sapphire's treacherous ass, but it hadn't crossed my mind that she might have a new face. Now I had a clue to move with.

"Do you know if any pictures of her exist?" I asked, kissing her on her neck and up to her jaw line.

"There are none, but I remember what she looks like and we can find a sketch artist."

My growing excitement translated quickly into me grabbing ahold of her ass and pulling her towards me faster.

"From now on, you stick with me, understand?" I asked, biting her neck.

"Y-yes, daddy, whatever you say."

# Chapter 5
## Destiny

"Did the bitch even get a lick in?" I asked, after Angel sat down and picked up the phone in the non-contact visiting room.

Free was holding the phone in between me and her so we could all talk at once. But at the moment, I knew she was silently evaluating our sister. Knowing she'd gotten into a fight, I'd expected to see some type of mark on her light-skin ass, but it was obvious she'd had a flawless victory. The only marks on her face came from fatigue, but the light in her eyes hadn't dulled and that was a good thing.

"You know I can handle my own. Big bitch or not, she ain't have nothing for me," Angel replied, cracking a smile.

"You gotta stay out of trouble," Free said.

"You know I didn't start it. Fat ass bitch ate my sandwich," Angel said, shaking her head.

I looked at Free and found her looking back at me, which meant we'd both heard the same thing just now.

"Did you say she ate your sandwich? Did you really just wax a bitch behind a state bologna sandwich, because I know you got plenty of commissary," I said in disbelief.

"It wasn't about the sandwich, it was about-"

"The respect," Free concluded, nodding her head in understanding.

When she put it like that, I had to understand because respect was demanded. We didn't accept less in the streets, so why would the jail be any different?

"You okay?" I asked.

"I'm maintaining. I won't lie to y'all, though, I'm scared."

Hearing those two words come from her mouth sent chills down my body. We'd all grown up under some of the worse circumstances imaginable. When you lived life on those terms, fear wasn't something you allowed to exist within. You did what you had to do without apology or hesitation because it was all about survival. To hear Angel say she was scared meant this situation she was in was a lot worse than Free and I had originally thought.

Looking at her now, I didn't see the 5'7" woman with the model looks and confidence, but instead I saw the 14-year-old girl who'd witnessed her older sister's first murder because a boy in school didn't know how to keep his hands to himself. Free had always protected us both, and Angel looked like she needed that now.

"Talk to us," I said.

"What can I say? I mean, the lawyer basically told me it's hopeless and I'm looking at the death penalty unless I snitch."

"We'll get a new lawyer and-"

"You know how good she is, Destiny. Free wouldn't have hired anyone who wasn't the best," Angel said softly.

When I looked at Free, the rest of my argument was swallowed because I could tell the lawyer wasn't the problem. We may not have known the full situation, but I could tell Free was analyzing, and she wasn't liking what she was coming up with.

"What exactly did Miranda say?" Free asked.

Before Angel spoke again, she looked around to see if any of the other bitches were paying attention to her instead of their own visit. But there were only two other people in the room and they were at least ten feet away."

"She said I could probably get around the shit at Burger King, but the problem was that same gun had been used in a previous shooting where twenty-four people died. Shit like that is viewed as a terrorist attack because of that Orlando night club shooting."

My first thought was *oh shit*, but I managed to keep my mouth closed and keep a straight face while continuing to process exactly what this meant. I almost asked why the fuck she still had that filthy ass gun, but knowing we were schooled in the same way, I knew she would've insisted on getting rid of it herself after the first situation. Twenty-four people though? The nigga Monster had been the target so how the fuck did twenty-three people fall with him?

"Twenty-four people?" Free asked, giving voice to my exact thoughts.

Of course, we all knew that we couldn't have this conversation here and now, but that question let Angel know that Free was pissed. By the look on Angel's face, I could tell she got the point.

"What did they charge King Deuce with?" I asked.

"I don't know yet. I'm waiting to get a letter back from him," Angel replied.

"Wait, you wrote him a letter?" Free asked in disbelief.

"Don't talk to me like I'm a dummy, Freedom. I know they read all our mail and I didn't say shit incriminating. I was just checking the niggas temperature."

"And you thought that was smart?" Free asked patiently.

"I thought it was necessary, considering that Miranda tried to get me to flip on him, which means his lawyer will probably do the same. She told me straight up that somebody gotta go down for this shit, and because of what happened back home, I don't look like the innocent Good Samaritan. I look like a part of the gang war."

Her statement painted an even clearer picture in my mind of how fucked up this shit really was, and I knew Free had to be seeing the same images in her mind. We'd all done plenty of dirt, but none of us had ever been this caught up.

"Five minutes," a cop yelled from somewhere unseen.

"I understand what you're saying, but I don't want you to do anything else," Free instructed.

"My preliminary hearing is in six weeks. Will I see y'all before then?"

"You call and we'll come, I don't give a fuck what Miranda has to say about it," Free replied empathetically.

"You know we got you, bitch, and you better not start crying," I said, forcing a smile on my face.

"Shut up. I ain't gonna cry. I wanna pray, though. Have you two been praying?" she asked.

Free and I both knew she was asking if we'd spoken to dad, and even though we hadn't, I knew we'd definitely have to after this visit.

"We will, sis, just hang in there and this will all be over soon," I said, putting my hand up to the glass separating us.

Free followed my lead and Angel completed the triangle by putting her hand between both of ours. No matter what we had to do, we'd get her out of this situation because her facing the death penalty meant that we were too.

"Stay strong. I love you," Free said.

"I love you, too," I said.

"I love you both. I'll call you soon," Angel replied, hanging up the phone.

We sat there and watched her be escorted out before we got up to leave. I don't know what Free was thinking, but I knew we had to figure out some way to get Angel the fuck out of there ASAP neither of us said a word until we were back in Free's Porsche 911 GT3, heading from Atlanta.

"We gotta get her out," I said.

"Don't you think I know that?"

If I hadn't noticed the frustration in her voice, the way she was shifting gears like she was trying to rip the stick out would've been a clear indication. It wasn't just the fact that Angel was in this situation, or our dad was halfway around the world, that had her feeling some type of way. It was guilt.

"It's not your fault," I said.

"Don't patronize me."

"I wasn't, I was telling you the truth. We all agreed to get dad out and that's what we were focused on, but sometimes shit happens. You were the first person to tell me that you can't plan for everything that could go wrong."

"Yeah, but-"

"But nothing, Free. Look, the more time you spend feeling guilty, the less you're focused on the real problems. Ain't no room for no pity parties sis, so I'ma need you to get your head in the game," I said seriously.

I could tell she wanted to blow my shit back, but she bit her tongue because she knew I was kickin' the real with her. We didn't lie to each other because the world offered us enough falsehoods. Lies would cause division, and nothing divided the Walker sisters.

It was a full half hour before either of us spoke again, both of us trapped in our own thoughts and trying to figure out how to end this nightmare.

"She ain't gonna get a fair trial. You know it's only a certain amount of time before she's linked to dad," I said.

"Especially with the gang angle of the situation she's in. They're just gonna think she's a chip off the old block."

"Plus, we're out here in Tennessee where it still ain't safe to be black in some spots. This is a bad situation, Free, what's our plan?"

"I'm working on it, just let me think. While I'm doing that you can get in touch with Kamile and let her know to have dad call us ASAP so we can bring him up to speed," she replied.

"Do you think it's a good idea to tell him everything? You know he's just gonna want to come back and get in the middle of this, and we can't have that."

"Do you wanna be the one to lie to Fathergod?" she asked, cutting her eyes at me.

"Touché," I replied, pulling my phone out and texting Ka-mile.

Keeping shit from Free was one thing, and I wasn't about to make a habit of that, but withholding information from my father was damn near an act of treason. As ugly as shit was we had to tell him.

"Okay, I sent the text, but you're gonna be the one to tell him," I said.

"Scary ass."

"You can call me what you want, but you didn't see the look on his face the last time I was the messenger," I replied.

"You can't see him through the phone, Destiny."

"No, but I can feel him. I love you to death, but you're taking this hit," I said stubbornly.

Despite the seriousness of the situation, I caught a smile creep across her face. We all know I was the youngest and therefore my daddy's baby, but Free had a special place in his heart that neither me nor Angel could touch. We weren't jealous because we understand that it came from a place of respect for the sacrifices she'd made to take care of us. She'd always be our protector.

"We gotta go underground," she said.

"Underground? Explain."

"We can't move with all eyes on us, and you know like I do that we're the only ones who can save Angel."

"Okay, but what's the plan? I mean, we can't pull a jail break because the feds are probably expecting that," I replied.

"They might be, and I'm not saying that's what we're gonna do. All I'm saying is that we've gotta get out of Atlanta unde-tected because I can't fucking think or plan with the law watching my every move."

"I can dig it. So how are we gonna disappear?" I asked.

"Well, the cleanest way I can think of is to have a moving company show up like they're packing up someone in Angel's building and we vanish with the furniture."

"Moving company? So, you must be thinking about our cousins Tiny and the Trans Atlanta company he works for. An out of state move?" I asked.

"Yep. I'm thinking we head further south where we can blend in better since spring break is still going on."

"I'll text him now and find out where he's at. Are we gonna have the rest of the team meet us down there?" I asked, texting Black Sam first to let her know we'd be there soon.

"Yeah, we're all going underground because a storm's coming. I want my sister and I'll kill everything standing in the way of that."

Aryanna

# Chapter 6
## Angel

One week later…

"I brought you breakfast, Walker."

Ordinarily, that statement wouldn't invoke the fear I was currently feeling, but the problem was that the officer wasn't standing at my door with the tray on my food slot. He was in my room. Mentally I was kicking myself in the ass because I'd broken one of the Cardinal Rules of incarceration and slept through the sound of my door being opened.

The officer standing in the middle of my cell worked third shift, and he was definitely a weird one. He looked like your average white dude with brown hair and brown eyes, about 5'10", weighing maybe one hundred eighty-five pounds, not unattractive, but not my type. And the way his flashlight always lingered too long when he was walking past my cell during his rounds at night made me uneasy.

In these blue jail issued scrubs with my hair in a ponytail, I knew I didn't look like nothing. But the way dude watched me, you would've sworn I was putting on a peep show for him. And now he was in my cell.

"Wh-what time is it?" I asked, sitting up and feigning like I was trying to organize my thoughts, but I was already thinking at the speed of a light.

"It's a little after 5am."

"Breakfast ain't until 6am, and normally it's served by first shift. What's this?" I asked, accepting the Styrofoam container he handed me.

"I wanted you to have some real food and not the slop they normally give you."

When I opened the container, I found an omelet that made my mouth water instantly, grits, along with a couple sausage links, a few strips of bacon, and some toast. As bad as I wanted to dig in, I could hear the faint warning bells in the back of my mind because wasn't shit free.

"So, what's this for?" I asked, looking up at him.

"Nothing, I just figured you'd be tired of eating that bullshit they feed you from the kitchen. I'll give it to somebody else if you don't want it, though," he replied, extending his hand to accept the tray back.

My intentions were to hand it back, but two weeks of living on junk food had my stomach growling for the meal in front of me. Picking up the fork in the container, I got down to business like a big bitch at a buffet.

"Home cooking is good for the soul," the officer said, chuckling.

I was so engrossed in the meal that I'd forgotten he was still standing there. But now that I noticed him, I was wondering why he was still there.

"Uh, thank you," I said, hoping he'd get the hint that it was weird to watch me eat.

"Oh, it's my pleasure. Try the omelet. I made it with green peppers, onions and mushrooms."

"That sounds good, but I don't eat mushrooms," I replied truthfully.

"Well given your situation, I don't think you can really be picky. Plus, it seems unappreciative."

The change in his tone was slight, but still noticeable. It gave me a bad feeling.

"I do appreciate all the trouble you went through, but I'm allergic to mushrooms and that's why I don't eat them," I said.

"Allergic to mushrooms? You wouldn't be lying to me would you, because I didn't see that anywhere in your file?"

"My-my file," I repeated slowly.

"Maybe you should just try it. I'm sure it won't hurt you."

Suddenly my appetite vanished, and now the growling in my stomach was definite fear. My instincts were telling me that my original impression of dude being 'off' was one hundred percent right, but I was in a no-win situation.

"I'm actually pretty full from the grits, sausage, bacon, and toast so-"

"Look, we can do this the easy way or the hard way," he said, all the politeness gone from his voice along with any pretense about him not expecting something in return.

"Do what?" I asked.

His response was to unzip his pants and pull his dick out for me to see.

"You're gonna do whatever I tell you to do. And you're not gonna scream or fight because if you do, I'll kill you right here."

As he stated that, he was slowly stroking his dick, but he hadn't moved towards me yet. Despite me being a virgin, the sight of a dick didn't scare me because, as a stripper, I'd seen plenty of them. But the look in his eyes did cause a touch of panic. I didn't doubt that he meant what he said, so the question was how did I get out of this situation without getting fucked.

"Listen I-"

"I didn't say you could talk, bitch. This ain't the time for words from your mouth because your mouth has more important business to attend to. Now we can do this with or without the handcuffs, but I promise you that if I feel so much as one tooth graze my penis, you're dead. So, do I need to handcuff you?" he asked, moving closer to me.

Common sense told me that if my hands were bound, I probably wouldn't be able to fight him off. It wasn't that he was so much bigger or stronger than me, but he had that look of madness in his eyes you might find in a rabid dog. He'd have to be put down before he'd quit fighting. And since I knew that, my decision was an easy one.

"No handcuffs needed, but I hope you know what you're doing. I'd hate to think this little encounter is gonna be all about you," I said, sitting the tray on my bunk.

"Trust me, you'll get yours. I just don't wanna cum too fast once I'm inside you, which is why I want my first nut to go down your throat. It shouldn't take long, and after that, I'ma fuck you good. I promise."

I gave him a slight smile as I spit in my hand and motioned for him to come closer. When I reached out and wrapped my wet hand around his shaft, I thought he might cum right then, if his breathing was any indication, but he managed to control himself.

Slowly I stroked him, feeling the tension release from his body as it rebuilt on the backbone of sexual desire. It didn't take a full minute before he was rock hard in my grasp. Then I felt his hand move to my head, pulling me towards him. With his dick in my right hand I opened my mouth wide like I was guiding him home. But right before his dick passed the threshold of my lips, I swung and uppercut to his nuts that would've made Floyd Money Mayweather proud.

I heard the air leave his lungs in a rush as he crumbled to the floor and vomited. I didn't waste no time or give two fucks about getting messy because within seconds I was on his back grabbing a fist full of his hair with my left hand while my right hand grabbed his chin. Using all my strength I twisted until I heard the sweet grindings of his neck breaking.

When I sat back on my bed, a wave of satisfaction rolled over me, but it only took a minute for me to realize how bad having a dead cop on my floor was. I mean, who would believe me when I told them what had really gone down in here? Every time I turned around I was making my situation worse. There was only one thing I could do now, though.

I calmly got up off my bunk and walked out into the day room, going straight to the phone because I was gonna need more than institutional help. I quickly dialed the number and listened to it ring seven times before a somewhat sleepy voice answered.

"Why you calling so early?" she asked, once the automated voice connected our call.

"Because I need you to get down here ASAP."

"Angel, my hours are-"

"Miranda, there's a dead cop on the floor in my cell. He sexually assaulted me, and in about twenty minutes the next shift is gonna notice he's not breathing. Get-the-fuck-down here," I growled, hanging up before she could say shit else.

I desperately wanted to call Free, but the message Miranda had brought me a couple days ago said that everyone would be out of reach for a while. At the time, I'd felt hope and even excitement because I knew that meant it was all hands on deck trying to get me out of this situation. Right now, I just wanted my big sister, though.

Obviously, this wasn't my first body, but damn was it a bad one to catch. As much as I hated to do it, I knew I had to go back into my cell, and I couldn't even take a shower because I knew some form of examination was gonna have to happen. Now I just had to figure out how I didn't get killed when the other cops found this mufucka in here.

My first thought was to just sit on my bed and wait for someone to come in, but then I'd probably be asked why I didn't scream for help after it was all over. If I was to be believed, I was gonna have to make a move quick. Walking back into my cell, I went straight to the body on the floor and grabbed the walkie-talkie off of his belt. After visiting my father for years in different institutions, I knew all officer radios came with a panic button in case some shit popped off and they needed help.

There definitely was no help for Officer Pervert, but I had no doubt that this would bring the troops. I hit the orange button on the walkie-talkie and then I sat down on my bed to wait. Instantly, there was chatter all over the radio about the emergency signal coming from the maximum-security floor, and the Calvary was definitely coming. In my head, I was counting, and I'd just reached the thirty second mark when I heard the lock turn in the front door and multiple footsteps approaching. I put the radio on top of what was left of my breakfast and put my hands in the air.

"What the fuck? Allen, Allen, are you okay?" asked the first cop through the door, rushing to the fallen cop's side.

Directly behind him was a short, white, blonde hair female with lieutenant bars on her uniform.

"Step out here and put your hands behind your back," she ordered, pulling a pair of handcuffs from behind her back.

I did as instructed, not even mad at the force she used when slamming me up against the wall right outside my door because with a female on the scene, I felt like I had a potential ally.

"He's not breathing Lieutenant," the other cop hollered from inside the cell.

"Call for medical," she ordered.

"Won't do no good," I said, truthfully.

"You better hope it does, Walker, or you won't have to worry about standing trial for your other crimes," she replied, in a threatening tone.

By now more cops were swarming the unit, but I didn't mind because hopefully the more witnesses to all this, the less likely the odds of a successful cover-up.

"Uh, Lieutenant, I think you should come in here," the cop in my cell called out.

"Watch her," the lieutenant ordered, passing me off to another cop.

As she stepped back into my cell, two nurses came through the front door and went in the cell right behind her. Of course, by now everybody in the unit was awake and at their doors, and I could hear bitches asking what was going on. Thankfully, Renata's big ass wasn't still in this unit because she would've been all up on the door instigating shit.

"Come with me," the lieutenant said, taking me back from the cop she'd handed me off to and leading me out the front door of the unit.

We were followed by one of the two nurses who had come to try and save the life of the dead cop, a young black chick with an average face and a big ole ass. I was led down the hall a little way before we stopped and I was forced to put my back up against the wall.

"What happened Walker?" the lieutenant asked.

For the first time, I looked at her name tag and filed the name T. House to my memory so I knew exactly who to send Miranda at.

"I think I should wait until my lawyer arrives before I answer any questions."

"Your lawyer? It could be a while before you get to make that phone call. Right now, I just need to know how my officer ended up face down in your cell with his neck broken."

"I already called my lawyer and she should be arriving shortly. Like I said, I think it's best that I wait on her to get here before I do any talking," I replied.

The frustration was written all over her face, but it wasn't affecting my decision. There was absolutely no benefit to me talking about a murder to the cops without my lawyer, especially when I was the only suspect.

"Okay, look, you don't wanna say shit, and I get it because you don't wanna incriminate yourself. I haven't read you your rights and you've asked for a lawyer twice, which Nurse Jackie here can attest to, if the need should arise. I'm just asking you, woman to woman, is it what it looks like?"

Right then I knew that for her to ask me that question meant the other cop had turned the body over and saw that ole Allen had died with his dick out. The cynical side of me wanted to believe this bitch was getting ready to try and push this shit under the rug, but the nurse standing next to us suggested otherwise.

"Yeah, it's what it looks like, but he didn't get what he wanted."

"And what did he want?" Lt. House asked softly.

"To cum down my throat and fuck me really good."

I'd halfway expected to find some doubt in her eyes when I spoke the truth, but I actually saw compassion instead.

"Okay. I know you don't wanna say too much without your lawyer, but I need you to go with this nurse so you can be examined."

"Yeah, and I bet while I'm gone you and your people will clean it up real nice so it looks like the whole situation is my fault," I said with blatant disgust.

"Everybody ain't out to get you, Walker, and I'm not gonna look the other way on this."

"If you really mean that then go back in my cell and get the tray of food off my bed," I replied.

I could see the question bubbling in her eyes, but she bit her tongue and went back in the unit.

"Don't worry, I'm not gonna let them get away with this shit. King Deuce is my nigga," Nurse Jackie whispered, giving me a wink and squeezing my shoulder reassuringly.

"Get word to him about what happened, and tell him that he knows I ain't gonna fold."

All she had time to do was nod because the lieutenant was back with the Styrofoam try in her hand.

"Okay, why is this so important?" she asked.

"Because he said he made it for me and he was nice until I told him I couldn't eat the omelet because of my allergies. I think he drugged the food."

"I'll bag it and have it tested, but I need something from you," she said softly.

"What's that?"

"Tell your lawyer to keep this quiet for the moment, and I'm not asking because I'm trying to cover this up. Just trust me, this could work out in your favor."

# Aryanna

# Chapter 7
### Fathergod

"Pray."

"Man, please, please let me go. I-"

"That ain't how you pray," I said, chambering a round into the head of my .40 Caliber Desert Eagle.

"Fathergod, I'm begging you to have mercy on me and my family. I swear to you that I don't know nothing."

I was hearing his words, but as I stood over the man kneeling before me, I was studying his eyes. Even the best liars couldn't keep the truth from swimming in their eyes, especially when in high pressure situations such as this. It turned out that Rochelle, aka Sweetpea, had been telling the truth the first night we'd met. And not only had she provided an accurate description of Sapphire's new face that was verified by her boss, but she'd also found one of the fed agents who'd done the transport. The only downside was that she'd lost her job because I'd had to have a rather serious talk with her boss. But she was rolling with Fathergod now, so it was all good.

I'd been tempted to bring her along on this excursion into Chicago's suburbs, but I'd had a feeling this visit with agent Latrell Fox might go the way it was going now. There I stood in the middle of his nicely decorated living room with my pistol pressed to his head while his wife, son, and daughter looked on. And he still chose to lie.

"It's already late, Latrell, and I've never been long on patience. I wanna know where you last took Sapphire. And what name is she living under now?" I asked.

"I-I don't know!"

You would think the sound of his wife and children crying would've motivated him to be a standup guy in that moment, and show his loyalty to them instead of the FBI. Maybe he just needed a little more motivation. Being that his wife, daughter, and son were kneeling just a few feet away from him, I only had to move my gun a short distance. As it landed on the little boy, who couldn't have been more than 6 years old, I saw Latrell open his mouth to speak, but his words were drowned out by the roar of the cannon in my hand.

I wasn't surprised when he lunged at me, and since I'd anticipated this move, it was easy to side step and smack him across the back of his head with the pistol.

"Bitch, if you don't shut up, I'ma drop your daughter next to your son," I warned the hysterical woman, who was trying in vain to put her son's thoughts back inside his head.

Oddly enough, the little girl just knelt there and stared me down with more hate in her eyes than I'd ever seen in one person, but there were no tears. I could tell she was a couple years older than her brother, but those eyes were light years ahead of their time.

"In case me and my associates haven't been clear, we're not here to play games with you. I don't give a fuck that you're a fed. I don't give a fuck that you have a family. The only thing I give a fuck about is the information I want. Now you can give it to me, or you can watch the rest of your family die," I said calmly.

"I-I don't know where she is. Once the surgeries were complete, the bureau got her out of town and relocated with her new identity. Th-there's not even a file on her because of how long your reach is. I swear, I don't know where she is. All I-all I know is that she has a son."

"What?" I asked, reaching down and pulling him up to my eye level by his t-shirt.

"She has a son. I don't know how old, but she had him sometime in between the first and second surgery."

"Who's the father?" I asked, feeling a sudden tightness in my chest.

My question wasn't answered immediately, but feeling the hot gun barrel under his chin properly incentivized him.

"The guy you murdered is the father," he replied.

I shouldn't have been surprised, or even upset after all this time, but it seemed like every time I turned this scandalous bitch was betraying me in another way. Without warning, I pulled the trigger, putting his brains on the ceiling before I turned the gun on his wife and daughter, and killed them too.

"Let's go," I said, dropping the body and addressing the two soldiers who had been silently observing the entire scene.

"You want us to burn the house down?" one soldier asked.

"Nah, get some people up here, clean up, and make the bodies disappear ASAP," I ordered, walking out of the house and climbing into the back of the waiting Escalade truck.

"Take me home," I said, pulling my phone out and texting Sweetpea to meet me at my apartment.

We'd actually been spending a lot of time together, but I wasn't hitting her up tonight about no pussy. I wanted answers.

While I'd been taking care of business, I'd had my phone on silent, which was why I'd missed Kamile's call, and her text saying it was urgent that I call her left me feeling some type of way. Those few words sounded like bad news, and with the way I was already feeling, I didn't need any more of that. Still, I dialed her number and waited on her to answer.

"Where are you?" she asked immediately.

"On my way home, why?"

"I'll meet you there then so we can talk."

"Can it wait, I just told Sweetpea to come to the house so-"

"You can get your dick wet later Johnathan. Besides she's working and we're busy. So, I need her at the club," she said.

"I'll be home in thirty," I said, hanging up and texting Sweetpea back to let her know to be at my house in the morning.

I had no idea what Kamile was on at 1am, but I definitely wasn't for the bullshit right now.

I know she was a friend, and she'd been real helpful, but I'd still shoot her ass if she pissed me off tonight. It only took twenty minutes to get back to my apartment building, and I wasn't surprised to find Kamile waiting in the hallway for me. If she would've been late, I would've been pissed, and I liked that she was smart enough to be aware of that.

"So, what's so important that you had to rush right over here in the middle of the night?" I asked, pushing the button to summon the elevator.

"I'd rather have this convo where I can be sure the walls ain't listening."

"Well, after you," I said, stepping aside when the elevator doors swung open so she could go first.

Once we were on the elevator and the doors closed, the smell of her perfume smacked me in the face, and it was intoxicating. I could tell by her reflection off the elevator doors that she was all business, but I couldn't help noticing that she was all woman. Tonight, she had on a little black dress that stopped mid-thigh, with some purple high heels on that I knew would match the highlights in her hair under the right light. It seemed like no matter what she wore, she still looked damn good.

"Don't be staring at me like that as long as you are fucking Sweetpea," she said.

"I don't know what you talking 'bout, and you the one who sent Sweetpea my way."

"That's because my eyes ain't the only ones who see those cameras, and it would've looked real crazy for y'all to be sitting in the boom-boom room talking. That didn't mean you had to turn one night into a love affair."

"Jealous?" I asked, as the doors swung open.

The look she turned to give me said 'nigga please' in any language, and it made me laugh. Leading the way out of the elevator into my basement apartment, I was still smiling, but I hadn't overlooked the fact that she hadn't given me a verbal response.

"You want a drink?" I asked, going to the kitchen.

"Shot of Henney, no ice."

I grabbed the bottle I kept in the freezer and two shot glasses. I returned to the living room to find her sitting on the couch.

"So, what's up?" I asked, pouring us both shots.

"Your daughters wanna talk to you."

"Okay, what's the problem with that?"

"The problem, Johnathan, is that they think you're halfway around the world, so we're gonna have to make the call on three-way," she replied, before downing her shot and refilling it herself.

"A'ight, we can do that. You act like it's a big deal or something."

"It is a big deal because I don't like lying to them, and I told you that. This shit could backfire, Johnathan, and I'm telling you that it's gonna be bad my nigga."

"Listen-"

"Nah, you don't get it because you been gone. I'll be the first to admit that all your daughters are strong, intelligent, and capable at anything they set their mind to. But they still need you. To go so many years without having you, and then to know you're out but can't be with you has to be fucking with them. If you get caught up it could destroy them," she said sincerely.

Part of me wanted to tell her that she didn't know what the fuck she was talking about, but the reality was that she might know my daughters better than me in some ways. That was hard for me to admit.

"I can't leave now, I just found out some more info about my baby mama."

"I understand you need to see this thing through, but it might cost you too much. I don't know exactly what's going on with Angel, but I know Freedom has taken her whole team off the radar, which means she's planning something. Any moment she could show up in Chicago, and this city ain't big enough for the three of you. You know they can't focus on Angel if they're worried about you."

It wasn't a child's job to worry about their parents, but I knew my girls did just that. It didn't matter how long I'd been gone because the bond we had would never be broken, and I cherished that.

"I can't leave, Kamile, so what do you suggest? Should I come clean and tell them that I'm still in the country, even though it will distract them?" I asked.

For once, she wasn't quick to respond, instead choosing to throw back a shot and quickly using another one to chase it.

In a perfect world Angel would be out, Sapphire would be dead, and we'd all be in a country without extradition living the good life. That reality was a long way away, and having to admit that made me pick up the bottle of Hennessey and take a long swig. I needed to come up with a plan.

"I don't know the answer to that question, Johnathan, but you've gotta figure something out before people die who don't need to," she said.

"So, what if we combined our resources?"

"What exactly do you have in mind?"

"I don't know where in the country my baby mama is, but I know she was in Chicago at least nine or ten years ago, which means somebody here has to know something. Plus, if she's feeding the feds information, she has to somehow still be in contact with my homies in some way. I've already sent the word and her picture to the council so everyone could be on the lookout. But if the indictments are coming down, then it's too late," I said, shaking my head.

"I don't see how I can help. I mean, you're completely connected with the Black Guerilla Family so..."

"Yeah, but you got hoes and plenty of neutral niggas around the city, which means you can get answers that I can't. Sometimes you gotta use finesse instead of force, feel me?"

"Alright, so what did you find out about her today?" she asked.

Before I could answer that, I had to take another long drink of the potent liquid, hoping it would wash away the taste in my mouth from the words I was about to speak.

"I found out she got another kid, a little boy."

"Yours?" she asked, eyebrows raised.

"Nah, the bitch ass nigga she tried to have kill me that night. Dude's name was Rodney and he was a dope boy from Zone 6 in Atlanta. The problem with a nigga that lacks versatility and only knows how to sell dope is that he wants to sell it everywhere he can. As you can imagine, the nigga started pushing his product in my territory, and since I wasn't going for it, a war started. I don't know how she met that nigga or when they started fucking, but the dick was good enough for her to sneak that mufucka into our house, where our daughters slept, to body me. Only problem was they both forgot that every closed eye ain't sleep. I thought I killed them both."

"I see why you wanted to now. That was some low down dirty shit your baby mama did," she replied, holding out her shot glass for a refill.

I topped her off and then sat the bottle on the coffee table between us because I could feel the liquor kicking in.

"How old is the little boy?" she asked.

"He can't be no more than ten years old."

"Do she got any family she could stash him with because that could flush her out and-"

"Nah, she ain't got no family. All we had was each other," I said bitterly.

There was no doubt the shit Sapphire did was fucked up, but what stuck with me was how she'd played me for a fool both before the failed hit and now, knowing she'd been alive while I served time for her murder.

"I know you wanna kill her, but you can get your sentence reduced if you produce her to the general public alive."

"It wouldn't change the fact that I killed ole boy, and you better know the government ain't about to let me air their dirty laundry. I'd be dead quicker than you could say conspiracy," I replied, shaking my head again.

"Well then I guess we need to find the bitch and put an end to all this shit. And we need to do it fast because I don't take days off of work, not even for you."

"I hear you, boss lady. You get with your people and I'll get with mine, and hopefully we can get this done before my daughters show up on your doorstep."

"Agreed. I'll call you in the morning Johnathan, make sure you're available and not stuck in between Sweetpea's legs," she said, standing up and heading for the door.

"Jealous?" I asked again.

She stopped in her tracks, turned around, and walked back over to me.

"I have no need to be jealous," she replied bending down so she could whisper in my ear.

"If I wanted you, I'd have you, and trust me my pussy is better than hers and more than you've ever dreamed about."

No woman had ever gave me chills, but watching Kamile Armstrong walk away from me did that and more.

# Chapter 8
### Freedom

"I don't wanna hurt you, babe."

"You won't," I replied, grabbing him by his dick and pulling him down on top of me.

There had been six of us cramped into a two-bedroom apartment for the first few days we'd been on the move, which meant no privacy at all. Now that we'd reached our destination of Miami, Florida, and we had a three-bedroom beach house, I was determined to get some dick.

It was still crowded in this mufucka, but Bone and I had our own room with a lock on the door, and I wasn't taking no for an answer. As soon as the head of his dick was inside me, I felt my whole-body tense while my pussy grabbed him like a life preserver.

"Oh damn," he moaned, once he was all the way in.

I knew he needed a moment to gather himself, but I couldn't wait. Wrapping my legs around his back, I brought us closer, my mouth finding his in the dark so we were completely joined together. I could still feel his hesitation in the tentative strokes he was giving me, but it had been so long since I'd had sex that I still came all over him within minutes. That was all the permission he needed because then he was putting his back into the blows he was delivering, and I loved it.

"Fuck me, nigga," I demanded, lifting my hips into his downward force and causing a collision that made my eyes lose focus.

Before I knew it, he'd backed up, put both of my legs on his shoulders, and was giving me long dick at a steady rhythm.

"Bone, I-I oh god I-"

My orgasm came before the words could leave my mouth, rocking my body hard enough to make me question my sanity.

Each time I came, my pussy became more sensitive and so with each stroke I could feel him throbbing inside me. The sounds of wetness in the air were like a tropical storm, and I could tell they were motivation for him.

"Hands and knees," he demanded, backing up enough to allow me to move into position, and then he was right back inside me.

He tried to drive my head through the wall with his first blow, but I was smart enough to brace myself for that while still managing to throw that ass back at him.

The feeling of his fingers digging into my hips while he pounded me gave me a sensation beyond description. And when he finally came inside me, I found that world tilting orgasm I'd been chasing. We both collapsed on the bed, fighting for oxygen, but satisfied beyond words.

"Y-you okay?" he panted, reaching for my hand.

"Uh huh."

"You sure, babe?"

This time when he asked, he pulled me towards him and put his hand on my stomach.

"I-I'm fine, the baby is fine, and the pussy is excellent," I replied, laughing and laying my head on his chest.

"You damn sure right about that. I mean, it's always been fire, but it seems like it's got levels to it now. After you came twice, I damn near lost my mind."

"They say pregnant pussy is the best pussy. Shit, wait 'til I'm like eight months, you might drown," I said, laughing softly.

I'd expected some type of smartass retort, but he was silent. I could hear his heart beating steadily, almost at a normal rhythm now that the festivities were over, but louder than that were his thoughts.

"Babe, talk to me."

"What do you want me to say, Free? You know I'm worried, just like how I know this is something we have to do."

"It's all going to work out," I said, snuggling closer to him.

"I know."

I didn't feel like he doubted what he said, but his tone made me wonder what would happen if everything didn't work out. If something happened to our child because of the stress and drama that surrounded me and my family, I feared it might cause division between us. I didn't even want to think about that because I loved this man in a real way, and I couldn't choose between him and whatever had to be done for my family.

"Whatever happens, I know you're gonna be right by my side the whole way."

I don't know what made me speak those words because even I could hear the insecurity in them, but a part of me needed to check his temperature.

"You know I got you," he replied, kissing me on the forehead.

"And I got you," I said, taking is dick in my hand and stroking it slowly.

One of the many things I loved about him was the short amount of time it took him to rejuvenate. It only took a few moments for him to come to life in my hand.

"Baby, we can't-"

I silenced his protest by rolling on top of him and sliding him right back into his favorite spot. In that position, we remained until the night collapsed on itself and daylight was allowed its turn reign supreme. After sunrise, we both fell asleep, but the sound of banging on the bedroom door interrupted us.

"What?" I called out, slightly cranky.

"Dad's on the phone," Destiny yelled.

Quick as a cat I hopped up, threw on some shorts and a t-shirt, and ran for the living room.

"Put it on speaker," I said, sitting on the couch next to Destiny.

"We're here, dad," Destiny said.

"How you holding up?"

"We're good, how about you?" I asked.

"Sweetheart, you know I'm fine so please do no unnecessary worrying about me."

"I'm not, it's just-"

"Destiny, look at your sister right now and tell me if she's got those three wrinkles in her forehead, and don't lie," he said.

I tried to quickly relax my face, even though I had no idea how to do that, but I wasn't quick enough because Destiny started laughing immediately.

"How'd you know, dad?" Destiny asked.

"Because I know my daughters. Now I'm gonna say this again, and you know how much I hate to repeat myself, but you two don't need to worry about me. Tell me what's going on with you."

For a moment, both of us just looked at each other, waiting on the other to speak while trying to formulate the right answers.

"What do you mean?" Destiny asked.

"Well, for starters, y'all got in touch with Kamile and said you wanted to talk to me. I could assume that you just missed my voice. But considering the fact that you've gone underground, I'm sure it's more than that."

Again, Destiny and I looked at each other, but neither of us was really surprised because our father always knew everything.

"We're going after Angel,' I said,

"Yeah, I figured that. Do you have a plan? I mean, other than to bury everything standing between you and her?"

"I'm working on it," I replied, defensively.

"Don't get testy. I know you have a shoot first ask questions last outlook on my situations, but they'll probably be ready for that."

"If they want a war, I'll give it to them," I replied.

"And who wins in that situation? As a family, we'll do whatever has to be done, but the goal is for all of us to be together in the end, and not just at someone's funeral," he said.

I knew he was right, but I'd put a hole in the world before I let them people put my little sister on death row.

"Have you talked to Angel?" he asked.

"Yeah, we went to see her," Destiny replied.

"And?"

I knew we'd get around to this question and I figured since Destiny had done so little talking she could handle this question. I motioned for her to speak, but her response was to sit back on the couch and cross her arms over her chest. Girl was more stubborn than any donkey.

I quickly relayed the conversation we'd had with Angel, hating the sound of the words 'death penalty' as they came out of my mouth. When I finished, everyone was silent, but I knew what my father was gonna say.

"I'll be there in a couple of days."

"Johnathan, you can't do that, we already talked about this."

"Who was that?" Destiny asked.

"Kamile, is that you?" I asked, wondering if she'd been on the phone the whole time, and why she hadn't said shit.

"Yeah, it's me. Johnathan, did you hear what I said?" she asked.

"Yeah, I heard you, but-"

"Then you know you can't do what you're thinking," Kamile said.

I didn't know when the fuck Kamile had got so familiar with my father to have conversations with him about the moves he should and shouldn't make, but she was doing too much right now.

"Kamile you know we fuck with you and all, but this is a family conversation," I said with a slight attitude.

"I know that, and if I didn't fuck with all of you, then I wouldn't care if your dad came back. You know like I do that that's not the right decision, though. The right decision is to be patient until that window of opportunity opens. Meanwhile, you've got other things to focus on, Johnathan."

"Like what?" Destiny asked.

"Like finding your mother," he replied.

I could hear the hate in his voice when he made that statement, and it caused me to agree with Kamile because if he was still in the country he'd be tearing shit up to find her. Everyone knew that Fathergod could destroy the world.

"How you trying to find mom from where you at?" Destiny asked.

"I got the homies on it, but you two can help."

"How?" I asked.

"I need that tech support because you know I don't know shit about all that," he replied honestly.

"Destiny find a pen and piece of paper," I ordered.

Black Sam was the best at what she did and my dad knew that without me telling him because we'd used her when planning his prison break. In this day and age, any criminal enterprise had to have someone who could command cyberspace. It was mandatory.

"What you need dad?" Destiny asked, sitting back down with a pen and paper at the ready.

"I need a listing of all the judges and federal prosecutor who handle RICO cases in Chicago."

"RICO? As in the Racketeering Influenced Corrupt Organizations Act?" I asked.

"Yeah. If your mom is helping to bring down the BGF, then there's a pending RICO case against them, and the feds have to know where she is. I'm gonna work backwards."

"Do you think she's in touch with your homies?" I asked.

"I've put the word out, but she knows a lot of shit about me that has no statute of limitations."

I knew what that meant and it just further pissed me off that my own mother was on this type of bullshit.

"What happens if you find her?" Destiny asked.

To me that seemed like a dumb ass question because I knew my father, and any love I'd had for my mother had died when the whole truth had come out. I couldn't speak for how Destiny felt, though.

"That's not a conversation that needs to be had at the moment." Kamile interjected.

The look on my sister's face said she was about to have words with our dear friend, but I shook my head at her to prevent an unnecessary argument.

"I'll put my people on it, dad, and I'll be in touch as soon as I know something," I promised.

"Okay. You two take care of each other and be safe out there. I love you both."

"I love you, too, daddy," we said in unison.

When the phone went dead we both just sat there for a minute, each trapped in our own thoughts.

"I miss him so much," I said.

"I know, me too. Why didn't you tell him you're pregnant?"

"Because that would've given him even more reason to come back. You know how protective he is, so imagine how he'd be knowing I'm carrying his first grandbaby," I replied.

"True. He's gonna kill her, huh?"

It would've been dumb of me to ask who she was talking about, so instead I studied her face for a moment in hopes of gauging how she was feeling.

"I think you know the answer to that," I replied neutrally.

Whatever she was feeling wasn't on the surface, but whatever she was feeling she was entitled to feel.

"I'ma take this to Sam," she said, leaving me sitting on the couch with my own thoughts.

I knew my father was gonna kill Sapphire if he ever found out where she was, and I was okay with that. I wouldn't force that view on either of my siblings, though.

"I need your help," Bone said, coming up behind me.

"What's up?"

"Come," he said, extending his hand and leading me to the kitchen.

There was a breakfast bar attached to the kitchen and that's where he led me. He pulled out a bar stool and sat me down.

"What do you need me to do?" I asked.

"Just sit there and look beautiful while I make us some breakfast."

"You might have to make that breakfast to go," Black Sam said, coming into the kitchen with Destiny trailing behind her.

"What are you talking about?" I asked.

"Miranda sent a message through our dummy Facebook page summoning you back to Tennessee, but there was no explanation as to why," Destiny said.

"She has no idea where in the world we are. We just told her we had to go out of town for a little while. If she's telling me to come up there, something must be wrong," I said, going to retrieve the phone off the living room table so I could call her.

"You think her phone is tapped?" Bone asked.

"Legally it would be extremely difficult to tap a lawyer's phone, but illegally…" Black Sam replied, allowing us to draw our own conclusions.

In that moment, it was worth the risk because from the sounds of it, we were getting ready to be on the move anyway. I quickly dialed her number and waited impatiently for her to answer.

"What's wrong?" I asked as soon as I heard her voice.

Listening to the words coming from her mouth, I felt my body go numb as pure rage took ahold of me. I had a million questions, but I didn't interrupt because I didn't want to miss a word of what I was being told.

"Submit the paperwork, I'll see you in twelve hours and we'll be ready within thirty-six," I said, disconnecting the call.

"What's wrong, Free?" Destiny asked, studying my face intently.

"A cop-a cop tried to rape Angel. She killed him."

"What?" Destiny exclaimed, her eyes matching everything I was feeling.

"I heard you move our time frame up, what's the play?" Bone asked, coming to stand beside me.

"The cops don't want this to get out because of how bad it would look on an already allegedly corrupt department. Miranda and Angel have kept quiet about what really went down, allowing Angel to be charged with capital murder, and in exchange we get a window."

"A window? What do you mean?" Destiny asked.

"They've ordered Angel to have a psychiatric evaluation, and for a small fee, there's a Lieutenant on the inside who's gonna schedule the appointment for when we want it so we can get her out," I replied, already making a mental note of what had to be done.

"Okay, so let's pack up and get ready to move," Destiny said.

"Hold up, because we're not travelling together. You and I need an alibi, Destiny, because we're already number one on the feds' list. This is gonna have to be done by Big Baby, Lil Boy, and Bone. And once they have Angel, we'll all meet up in Chicago so Kamile can get us out of dodge and back with dad."

"So, what are you gonna do?" Bone asked.

"With Destiny and I out in the open, it'll take the focus off of Angel. Destiny, I want you to throw a huge party, blast it all over social media and pick the hottest club in Miami. Black Sam, I want you to get me floor seats to a Warrior's game at home because I'm going to the west coast."

"You sure 'bout this, babe?" Bone asked.

"Yeah, I'm sure. Go get my sister, and don't get caught."

# Chapter 9
## Angel

Three days later…

"Walker, you need to get up and get dressed for transport. You've got ten minutes," the cop said, after banging on my door and disturbing my sleep.

After my meeting with Miranda two days ago, I'd been expecting to have to go out for my psych evaluation, but I didn't think it would be at the crack of dawn. I had no way of telling exactly what time it was because the cells in segregation didn't have windows. I just knew it was early because I hadn't even had breakfast yet.

Getting out of my bunk, I took the two steps to my toilet and squatted over the cold steel bowl, feeling more than just the relief from my bladder because this was the last time I would have to use this mufucka.

From the moment I'd looked in my sisters' eyes and told them how bad it looked, I knew they'd be coming to get me, and all I had to do was hold on. That hadn't been easy these last couple weeks, but it looked like it would work out.

After finishing up the task at hand, I went about the process of getting myself presentable for the world that awaited outside of these locked doors. I really wanted to talk to KD before shit went down, but to send him a message would've put my whole situation in jeopardy,

Once I was out, I'd instruct Miranda to tell his lawyer that it was okay to blame me for everything, and hopefully that would buy his freedom. If shit was different, my sisters and I would find a way to get him out. But after this move, there was no way we could stay in the country. I felt no disappointment about that, though, because the only man I'd ever loved was waiting for me somewhere out there. I'd just finished brushing my teeth when the lock on my door turned and it was pulled open by a familiar face.

"I brought you a tray, nothing fancy, and no date rape drugs included," Lt. House said, stepping into the cell and passing me the Styrofoam tray.

"Thanks, I probably won't eat though."

"I know, I just needed an excuse to come see you," she replied, whispering.

My first thought was that I'd counted my chickens before they hatched and now I was gonna be forced to sit and wait longer.

"Is something wrong?" I asked.

"No, everything is straight. I'm sorry you had to go through what you did, but everything will work out for the best."

It was on the tip of my tongue to tell this bitch that we weren't friends, nor could she understand what I'd been through, but I didn't give a voice to those words. Maybe part of her had an issue with sexual assault for personal reasons, or maybe she just saw a situation where she could capitalize financially. I didn't know so I wouldn't speak on it, and I damn sure wasn't about to jeopardize my shot at freedom by being judgmental.

"I appreciate that you did. Do you know exactly how this is gonna play out?" I asked.

"No, and I didn't wanna know. My job ended at setting your appointment up, the rest is on your people."

"None of this will come back to you, right?"

"As touched as I am that you're worried about me, you can rest assured that my tracks are well covered. I ain't going down for some cop not keeping his dick in his pants any more than I am you and whatever is gonna happen. Besides, I got the distinct impression that your people aren't someone I want for enemies," she replied.

I had no doubt that Free had had a talk with the Lieutenant when the money exchange took place because she'd want her to know that if anything went wrong a lot of people would die, including her. We wouldn't just kill for each other, we'd destroy everything we could to make our point clear.

"I got the restraints, Lieutenant," a young cop said, stepping into the door way.

"I'll get her ready and do the strip search," she replied, extending her hands to take the waist chain, handcuffs, shackles, and security box.

"That's a lot of hardware," I commented.

"To prevent escape," she said, sitting everything on my bunk, and then going back to the door to pull it shut without locking it so the dude in the hall wouldn't get a free peek.

Sitting the tray down I started to pull my shirt over my head, but she motioned me to stop and don't talk. After watching the hallway for a few minutes, she quickly moved to me and passed me a tiny key.

"It'll unlock the handcuffs and shackles, but you're gonna have to get the outside lock on the black security box off yourself. Hide it under your tongue," she instructed.

I did as told, and stood there patiently while she laced me with the jewels of bondage. This shit was anything but sexy though.

"Good luck," she said, before opening the door and escorting me out.

I was turned over to two cops I'd never seen before, but the look in their eyes was the same as a lot of men I'd seen. Thirsty. Ignoring them, I focused my mind on what would come after this and what plan my sisters had put together. Knowing them, they'd probably used the plan we'd never got to use on our dad, which meant a smash and grab job.

Once I was loaded into the cop car and we rolled through the gates of the jail, I kept my eyes wide open, hoping I'd be able to brace for impact so I didn't swallow the damn handcuff key.

I had no idea where this doctor's office was, but after forty-five minutes of driving, I was starting to wonder if a double cross was in play and I was about to disappear. Killing a cop hadn't exactly made me popular with his brethren. Luckily, before the thought of what these two cops might have in store for me had time to grow roots in my brain, we pulled up in the back of a three-story brick building.

As big as it was, I was sure there was more than a doctor's office inside, but obviously, the doctor was on the first floor. The cop in the passenger seat got out first, unholstering his police is-sued .357 Revolver while his eyes scanned the alley for anything out of place. A few moments later, he signaled his partner, who followed the same routine before opening the door and pulling me from the car.

One cop kept his eyes on our surroundings while the other one led me to the back door of the building and pushed the buzzer next to it. The sun was just starting to rise and so there were still shadows all around us.

When the back door opened, I was thankful for the semi-dark-ness because it hid the surprise on my face at the sight of Bone standing in front of me. The cop holding me by the arm didn't even get the chance to take a deep breath before the Berretta 9mm with the silencer coughed and splattered part of his face on me. Before he dropped I was already stepping to my right so Bone could move forward enough to dump two bullets into the face and neck of the other cop.

Without pausing, he quickly bent over the first cop and grabbed the ring of keys from off his belt, tossing them to Lil Boy as he came out of the back door.

"Put them in the trunk," Bone ordered.

I didn't get to utter a word before he scooped me up and threw me over his shoulder, carrying me into the doctor's office and taking me to an exam room.

"We need to be out of here in ten minutes," he said, sitting me back on my feet and disappearing back out the room.

It wasn't until then that I spotted Big Baby sitting in the corner of the room holding a blow torch.

"Big Baby, do you know what you're doing?" I asked warily.

Being that he didn't talk, I wasn't expecting a verbal response from him, but when a nigga that big and that black smiled the way he was right now, it was far from comforting.

"Just get the outside lock off. I've got a cuff key," I said, sliding it in between my teeth for him to see.

He nodded his head and I waddled over to him. Sparks were flying immediately and within minutes I was literally a free woman again.

"Thanks, bruh," I said, giving him a hug.

"Y'all done? Good, put these on," Bone said, coming back into the room and throwing me a duffel bag.

Once he and Big Baby left, I opened it to find some black sweat pants, a black t-shirt, a pair of cheap black sneakers, and a baby .380. I changed quickly, tucking the gun in my pocket just as a knock came at the door.

"You ready?" Bone asked.

"Yeah."

"A'ight, come on. We gotta get you out of here. Stuff everything into the duffel bag and let's roll," he said.

I did what he told me and followed him out into the waiting area where Lil Boy and Big Baby were waiting with a huge box that said Maytag appliances on the front, and a dolly.

"Damn, Lil Boy, you get taller?" I asked.

"Nah, you just shrunk 'cause you ain't been eating right. I'm still 6'7."

"Whatever, nigga. Okay, what's the plan now, and how did you three pull this shit off? Where are my sisters?"

"Can we save the questions for after we make a clean getaway?" bone asked.

"He's right, let's go. Angel, get in the box," Lil Boy commanded.

My first thought was to look at him like he was stupid, but I quickly remembered that this wasn't a nigga taking me out to dinner for two. With Lil Boy's help, I got inside the empty box and they wedged the flaps closed so you couldn't see down inside it.

It felt weird beyond words to be riding inside a box strapped to a dolly, but all I could do was hang on to the duffel bag and pray this nigga didn't dump me in the street. Without warning we hit a sharp incline, but just as quickly we came to a stop. Moments later, I heard the truck start and we were on the move.

Despite the confined space and stale air, I still took a deep breath as I began to relax, taking in the reality that I wouldn't die in some Tennessee prison. Now that I was out, I'd hold court in the street before I ever let them box me in again. Just when I was beginning to wonder how claustrophobic I really was, I felt someone tapping on the side of my hiding place.

"You comfortable or you wanna come out and play?" Bone asked sarcastically.

"Very funny, smartass, get me out of here."

Before I could object or scream, the box was pushed over and I rolled out onto the floor of an empty moving truck.

"You know I'll shoot you, right?" I said, dusting myself off and sitting up with my back against the wall.

"You love me too much to do that. Besides, that's just my way of saying I missed you," he replied, lighting a blunt and sitting next to me.

"You missed me? Now you know you ain't gotta shoot no shit my way."

"That's real talk. Me and your sister ain't never been the type to put no labels on shit, but that's my world right there, and that means you and Destiny are my sisters. Seeing Free hurt, hurts me. So yeah, I missed your ass," he said, passing me the blunt.

I hit that mufucka and I swear no weed had ever tasted sweeter. I smoked half the blunt in three pulls before passing it back, but Bone didn't complain.

"I missed you too, my nigga, and thanks for coming to get me. Not that I'm ungrateful or anything, but where the hell are my sisters?"

"They couldn't be part of this so they sent us while they established alibis for themselves. They're gonna meet up with us, though."

"And where exactly are we going?" I asked, accepting the blunt back.

"Chicago. We're gonna use the same connects Kamile used to get your dad set up in Russia."

"How is daddy?"

"As far as I know, he's good, but you know he was ready to come back into the country to get your ass."

Hearing that didn't surprise me in the slightest because there was absolutely nothing my daddy loved in this world more than his daughters. I couldn't wait until we were all together again.

"So, are we headed for Chicago now?" I asked, passing him the rest of the blunt to finish off.

"Yeah, but we'll get there before your sisters. Destiny is probably hung over from the major party she threw, and Free is gonna spend a few more hours on the west coast, being seen."

"Sounds like they had fun alibis. Are there any of those blankets or quilts moving company's use to make sure they don't bang people's shit up? I wanna make a little mat and lay down," I said.

"Sit here and fire up the next spliff while I do that for you," he replied, tossing an even bigger blunt in my lap along with a lighter.

I damn sure wasn't about to argue, so I put that bitch in the air. I was already feeling nice from the first one we'd smoked, but a few hits of the second one and I was in the nose bleed seats.

"I'll take that, and you can go hold that corner over there because you look good and fucked up," he said, lifting the blunt from between my fingers.

The ride in the back of the truck wasn't too rough, but I still didn't trust my legs, so I crawled to the corner. As soon as I got horizontal on top of the blankets, it was lights out. The way I went under, I felt like I hadn't slept in weeks, but I wouldn't complain because I needed it.

When you were locked up, you didn't really sleep you rested because you couldn't afford to let your guard down. After what happened with that cop, I hadn't got much rest either, though. I don't know how long I was out, but the minute Bone touched me, I was wide awake and reaching for the gun in my pocket.

"It's me, Angel," he said, holding his hands up.

"Sorry. Why are we stopped?"

"We're here. I'm dropping you off with Kamile and we're gonna go get rid of everything, but we'll be back," he said, opening the smaller door in the side of the truck.

When I got out, I spotted Kamile immediately, standing by the elevator. Looking around, I could tell we were in the parking garage of some high-rise building.

"It's good to see you," Kamile said, pulling me into her arms and hugging me tight.

"It's been way too long. I'm just glad you're seeing me out instead of having to visit me in prison."

"You know I love you, but Kamile don't do prisons so this is best for everyone," she replied, smiling at me.

"I ain't mad. But now that I'm out here in your world, can I get a hot bath and some real food, please?"

"Of course, and I've got a surprise for you," she said, pushing the button for the elevator.

"Oh lord."

Once the elevator arrived, we took it down to the bottom floor.

"Whatever happens, I need you to remain calm and don't panic," she said.

"Bitch, you better not have butt naked niggas waiting on me behind this door," I warned, laughing.

I thought she would've at least cracked a smile, but she didn't, and that made me nervous. As soon as she opened the door, I saw why.

"Da-Daddy? Daddy, what the fuck are you doing here?"

# Aryanna

# Chapter 10
## Destiny

"Yo, how are we still alive?" I asked in a whisper.

"I'm wondering the same thing. And why are you yelling?" Black Sam asked, moaning in obvious pain.

Somehow, we'd made it back to our hotel room and we'd managed to pass out side by side.

It might have been short notice, but I'd still thrown one of the biggest spring break bashes Miami had seen in ten years. At least that had been multiple people's post all over Facebook, Snap Chat, and Twitter. To be honest, my memory of last night was a little foggy because I'd been drunk off my ass, but it was still a damn good night.

"We need a drink," I said.

"Bitch, you must be crazy, I ain't ever drinking with your ass again. That's what got me feeling like death right now."

"The best way to cure a hangover is to drink. I'm telling you," I said, slowly sitting up and praying I wouldn't throw up.

So many mufuckas had vomited last night that it was unreal, but thus far I'd managed to hold the mixture of Bourbon and Vodka down.

Slow and steady I got up and made my way to the mini bar, reaching in with disregard for preference and grabbing the first two miniature bottles I could find. Wasting no time twisting off the first cap, I demolished the tiny bottle of gin in three swallows, immediately chasing it with the second bottle containing rum. The liquor hit my stomach with the force of an avalanche. But after a few moments, I felt a little steadier.

"Bitch, when did you undress me?" I asked, looking down at the purple bra and panties I had on, and then over to her laying there in her matching pink set.

"I thought I detected a draft," she said, running her hands up and down her body.

"Why are you rubbing on yourself with your eyes closed?"

"Stop being nasty, and my eyes are closed because it hurts to open them. Now, will you please stop yelling?" she said, whimpering.

The hangover was a mufucka, but the alcohol I'd just drank provided enough clarity for me to see her half-naked body for what it was. I'd had my eyes on her half-black half-Irish beauty for years, but Free always insisted that I keep it business. Free wasn't here now, though, and I knew Samantha was feeling me and wanted me to be her first woman.

"I know what will make you feel better," I said, moving towards her side of the bed.

"Pull out your gun and shoot me. That'll make me feel better."

Just the sight of her thick body was enough to have me feeling better. I'd only gotten to see how gorgeous she was when we facetimed, but the real thing was so much more than words.

Sitting beside her, I ran my fingers up and down her thigh gently, listening to her breathing speed up as I moved closer to her sweet spot.

When I pulled her panties to the side and stuck my middle finger deep inside her pussy, she quit breathing for a full ten seconds, and then she opened up her legs for me. I added my index finger to the mix and discovered how tight she was, but she was so wet that I knew she liked what I was doing to her.

My rhythm was slow, my touch was gentle, and little by little I felt her giving herself over to the moment. Once I knew she was knocking at the door to fulfillment, I stopped long enough to pull her panties off and get between her legs where I could complete my mission.

"Oh-oh god, I didn't know. D-Destiny I-I didn't know," she moaned passionately.

"Open up for me," I demanded.

Without hesitation, she grabbed her legs right behind her knees and spread wide for me. I licked her slowly and thoroughly, from the bottom of her pussy up to her clit and back. When I paused during my second trip and took her clit into my mouth, sucking on it with the force of ten vacuums, she came instantly. I drank her cum like champagne, continuing to lick and suck her in my quest for more. Fifteen minutes and two monstrous orgasms later, she surrendered and begged me to either stop or marry her. But I had no intentions on either until my phone started ringing.

"Yeah?" I answered breathlessly.

"We got her, time for you to get on the move."

"Okay," I replied, hanging up.

"Every-everything good?" Black Sam asked, panting and wiping the sweat from her face.

"Yeah, but we gotta go."

"Wait, I didn't get to taste you," she said, reaching for my hand.

"And that's not something I wanna rush… so are you coming with me or nah?"

"Hell yeah," she replied, getting up and getting dressed as fast as her head would allow.

I slipped back into my tan skirt and see through white blouse before calling downstairs and telling them to bring my car around. Once Sam had her booty shorts and tank top on, she grabbed our one suitcase out of the closet and made sure that anything belonging to us was in it.

"Here, drink this," I ordered, passing her a miniature bottle of Jack Daniels on my way to the bathroom, where I ran water over my phone and smashed it to pieces.

Once that was disposed of, I made sure to double check the hotel room in case we'd left anything behind.

"You good?" I asked, pulling on my all-white air force ones.

"I'm getting there. Why the fuck didn't you tell me you could eat pussy like that? You would've been got some of this shit," she declared, laughing.

"If I would've told you, you might've gotten scared, or you might've thought I was lying. I wanted it to be a surprise."

"Thank you, and I don't give a damn what Free talking 'bout because this only improves our business relationship. I'll do anything you want, bitch, I swear. Speaking of which, what's the plan now that I'm going with you?" she asked.

"You sure you wanna do that, Samantha? We're not coming back, so if you come with us, you're choosing a life on the run."

"I know what I'm choosing. I don't got no family left, and you all are like family anyway. So, tell me what our next move is."

"We'll discuss it in the car, let's go," I said, grabbing the suitcase and heading for the door.

By the time we got out front, my rented black 2016 Corvette was waiting, and once we were loaded up, I left a cloud of smoke behind us.

"We're gonna meet up with everybody in Chicago, but we're gonna take a detour into Key West and fly to Indiana. From there, we'll rent another car and drive the rest of the way," I said.

"You want me to get the plane tickets and rent the car?"

"Yeah, you can do that," I replied, aiming the car towards the highway so I could quickly put my old life behind me.

I'd miss getting money and causing havoc in the streets of Atlanta, but having my father and sister back was more than an even trade. Plus, everything about life was a hustle, so it was a guarantee that the Walker family would bounce back harder than ever.

"We gotta get you a new identity," I said.

"Don't worry, I've always got a coupe on standby just in case I gotta move fast," she replied, smiling.

I knew I liked her for more than just her pretty pussy. With the top down and the wind on our hair, we made the drive to Key West in about an hour and a half, which was perfect because we only had to wait another forty-five minutes for our flight to board.

I was too amped to sleep on the plane, but Black Sam put the two and a half hours in the air to good use, snoring and shit. It didn't surprise me that she was even more beautiful while she slept, but it did surprise me that I was actually watching her sleep. I wasn't the sentimental type to do no shit like that, yet there I was.

I damn sure wasn't ready to evaluate that any further, so instead I focused on the upcoming family reunion. It had been way too long since we were all together without the constant observation of C/O's and hating ass niggas, and I was looking forward to it. Once we got off the plane and into the terminal, we found the shuttle that would take us to the rental car place.

"Did you really rent this?" I asked, once we were standing outside and a forest green stretched hummer pulled up to the curb.

"Yeah, but don't worry, it comes with a driver."

Shaking my head, I climbed into the backseat and went straight for the fully stocked bar, selecting a bottle of strawberry Cîroc.

"Pour me a glass of that so I can get back to normal," Black Sam requested.

"I got you. Get the new phone out so I can call and let them know we're almost there."

While she went in the suitcase and got a phone out, I poured a healthy glass, but I kept the bottle for myself. We switched and I quickly dialed Kamile's number.

"We should be there in a couple of hours," I said once she answered.

"We? What do you mean *we*?"

"Don't trip, I got my girl with me and she's A-1. Plus, she's our tech support," I replied, winking at Sam.

"Okay, the first package is already here and the other should arrive at the same time as you."

"Is everything good?" I asked, wishing I could tell her to put Angel on the phone.

"Yeah, it's all good. Don't worry, just get here safe. I'll text you the address."

"A'ight, see you in a minute," I replied, disconnecting.

"Is Angel there?" Black Sam asked.

"Yeah, and Free should get there around the same time as us."

"Good, so we can relax and breathe a little easier now because the first leg of the journey is over," she said, extending her glass for a refill.

I topped it off before tipping the bottle to my lips and taking a long drink. I'd like to relax, but reality was that I couldn't do that until we were in Russian Airspace. Until then, anything could go wrong.

"Did you get any sleep on the plane?" she asked.

"No, I've got too much on my mind."

"I can tell. You look tense and stressed," she replied, sitting her empty glass back in the cup holder.

"What are you doing?" I asked, once she kneeled in front of me.

"Evening the score," she said, reaching beneath my skirt and pulling my underwear down until I raised slightly and allowed her to pull them off.

I started to open my mouth and insist that we wait, but before I knew it, she had my legs wide open with one on each of her shoulders. I may have been her first woman, but she licked my pussy like she knew it and she'd been there before. I barely had enough time to hit the buttons to put up the partition between us and the wide-eyed driver before I came. It was obvious she was enjoying herself because my climax didn't even make her pause.

"Y-you're good at this," I commented, searching for something to hold onto and anchor me to this world.

"I watch porn," she confessed, before going right back to work.

I didn't want to drown her, but my hands found themselves in her hair and I couldn't let go.

"W-w-wow," I exclaimed, when she gently bit my clit and made me cum hard enough to make me see stars on the back of my eyelids.

After my third nut, I made her 69 with me so we could please each other, and that was how we spent the first hour. Finally, when neither of us could take anymore, I made sure to give the driver the address we were going to, and we passed out in each other's arms. We stayed that way until the truck came to a stop in an underground garage and the door was opened for us.

"Make sure we got everything," I said, climbing out and feeling better than I had in a long time.

"I see you on your spoiled little rich girl shit," Kamile said, appearing out of nowhere with a smile on her face.

"It's good to see you, too," I replied, giving her a hug.

"Who's your friend?" Kamile asked, eyeing Samantha carefully.

"This my girl, Black Sam. Black Sam, this is Kamile."

They nodded toward each other, but neither offered a hand in greeting. Somehow Samantha's hand did end up in mine, but I didn't mind.

"Follow me," Kamile instructed.

We did just that and took an elevator to a basement apartment. As soon as the door opened and I saw Angel sitting on the couch, I ran straight to her, wrapping my arms around her tightly.

"I missed you so fucking much," I said, trying not to openly sob.

"I missed you, too, and I'm sorry I did that dumb ass shit."

"It's cool. We just ain't making no more moves that ain't calculated fully. Soon as Free get here, we gotta make our move to meet up with dad because-"

"You ain't got far to go," a voice said from behind me.

Deep down I knew who that voice belonged to and that had the excitement inside me bubbling, but the fear and anger quickly overtook that. Slowly, I turned around to face the man who was larger than life.

"Daddy, what are you doing here? Kamile, what the fuck is my father doing here?"

"I'm here because I wanna be. It's not her fault. Just give me a minute and I'll explain everything to you."

"You should wait," Kamile said, looking at her phone.

"I just got word that Free is here."

# Chapter 11
## Fathergod

The love I have for my daughters can't be put into words and I knew they felt the same way about me, but the look on Destiny's face said that she was pissed. I understood because Angel had been the same when she first arrived, and truthfully she was still a little mad, but her reasons were different now. She knew what my next move was.

At the sound of the front door opening, I turned around and came face to face with my oldest daughter and her entourage. In a split-second, I saw several different emotions flash in her eyes. But just as quickly, her poker face was intact.

"I'm listening," she said, coming all the way into the apartment and walking past me to hug Angel.

"Excuse me?" I replied.

"I said I'm listening, dad, because I'm assuming that after all the shit we've gone through to get you out of prison and keep you out that you have a good reason for being in Chicago."

"I... What the fuck happened to you?" I asked Kamile, as she came through the door behind a nigga that was damn near 7ft, holding her bloody nose.

"It's 2017 and the messenger gets shot, too. In her case, I made an exception because I like her, but the bitch still lied to me. Don't worry about her, though, you owe us an explanation," Free said, sitting on the couch next to her sisters.

To prevent my initial reaction, I had to bite a hole in my damn tongue because I knew I was wrong for being dishonest with them. This was the one and only time I was gonna be talked to like I was the child and they were the parents.

"I know I was wrong for allowing you to believe I was in Russia, but you can't be mad at Kamile because she's been trying to get me to leave since day one. You know how stubborn I am.

The reason I didn't leave is because I wanted to be closer by in case you needed my help getting Angel out… and because I gotta settle the score with Sapphire."

"Sapphire? You gonna risk your life for the same bitch who…"

"That bitch is our mother, Freedom, or have you forgotten that part?" Destiny asked.

"Our mother? My nigga, I'm your mother! I was there for you whenever you needed something. I put my life on the line every day for you. She's the one who destroyed our goddamn family so fuck that bitch 'cause she ain't no mother of mine," Free raged.

"I'm just saying, Free-"

"Man, fuck what you saying because-"

"Stop fighting," Angel yelled, silencing both of them immediately.

"We ain't never fought about this woman, not once in all the time we thought she was dead. The facts remain the same. She did what she did to us and dad. Destiny, I don't know if her being alive makes you feel some type of way, but you need to understand that Sapphire don't give a fuck about you," Angel said.

"Angel, you don't know what she was thinking then or what she's thinking now," Destiny replied.

"If she was thinking about you at all, then why has she never been here? Why did Free have to raise us? It wasn't Sapphire who taught you how to use a tampon. It was Free. It wasn't Sapphire who taught you about sex. Again, it was Free. And it damn sure wasn't Sapphire who taught you how to navigate the streets of ATL so you would not only survive, but get that money. It was Free. Sapphire started over and had a son. She's his mother, not yours," Angel concluded.

"A son?" Free and Destiny said at once.

Angel said no more and simply looked at me to explain. Being that I'd spent more time with her, she'd gotten answers and information that my other girls hadn't, but I could tell by the looks on their faces that they were gonna take it just as hard. I wouldn't lie to them, though, because when it came to this, they deserved the truth.

"Kamile and I have had our ears to the street since I've been out here and we learned that after all that shit went down ten years ago, Sapphire was in Chicago to get a new face. Of course, there are no pictures, but we got a description because she had several procedures due to the burns she got in the fire. The information we gathered led me to the fed who was Sapphire's transportation at the time. He couldn't tell me where she was located, but he did tell me she'd given birth to a son."

"H-how old?" Destiny asked.

"Nine or ten from what I was told," I replied softly.

I could see the hurt in my baby's eyes, and it was even more fuel to the hatred I felt for the woman who'd put it there. No matter how fucked up shit had been between us, our daughters hadn't deserved the treatment they'd gotten. Karma was coming though.

"Who's his father?" Free asked.

"The fed said it's the dude I killed that night."

"So, what's your plan dad?" Free asked calmly.

"Well hopefully, with your tech support, I can get the information I need and then go after her. Beyond that, I can't really say."

"I think you need to let your homies handle it and we all need to be on the next thing smoking," Angel stated.

"I agree with her," Kamile said, still holding her head back to stop her nose from bleeding.

"This ain't business, it's personal, and I'm not leaving until it's dealt with. You three will be leaving, though," I informed them.

I halfway expected an argument or some form of protest, but nobody said nothing. They just looked expectantly at Free. When her eyes locked with mine, I saw so much of myself that it was scary. I'd always taught all of them to take care of themselves and each other, but it wasn't until that very moment that I understood Free was the female version of me.

"Kamile, I want you and Free to get together and make the travel plans so-"

"No," Free said defiantly.

"No? Have you forgot who you're talking to? I let that shit slide earlier because I did owe you an explanation, but I'm still your father and my word is still law."

"On most days I would agree, but not today. You're my father and I'll always respect that. I just can't let your word overrule common sense. You know as well as I do that two heads are better than one, four are better than two, and on and on it goes. Right here in this living room is a better team than you or Kamile could assemble, and they're all motivated by the right thing. Family first. So, we're not going anywhere until the hunt for Sapphire is over with."

"Freedom?" one of the men she'd come in with called out.

I didn't know who that nigga was, but the way he felt about my daughter was written all over his face.

"Bone, we'll talk about this later."

"No, this is obviously a conversation we need to have now because you ain't thinking straight," he said, moving towards her.

I made a move to interrupt him, but Free threw her hand up and shook her head at me. When I looked at her, I saw that the hollow look devoid of emotion was gone and love was all over her face.

"Baby, I've done everything you've asked me to, but you can't ask me to keep allowing you to put yourself and our child in danger," he said.

"Wait, what? What child? Free, what's this nigga babbling about?" I asked, confused.

In response to my question the look on her face changed once again, and now she was my little girl who'd been caught doing something she wasn't supposed to.

"I-I'm pregnant daddy," she declared somewhat sheepishly.

When I opened my mouth to speak, no words came out. In my mind, I knew all of my daughters were old enough to be fucking, but no father is prepared to come face to face with that. Not only was she telling me she was pregnant, but the mufucka who'd done it was standing right in front of me.

"Dad," Destiny said, in a warning tone.

At first I didn't know why she had a look of worry on her face until I felt the weight of the pistol in my hand. Consciously, I didn't remember reaching for it, but now that it was in my grip, it didn't seem like a bad idea.

"Let me talk to you," Kamile said, taking me by the arm and pulling me into the back bedroom.

"What?" I asked, when the door was closed.

"Your daughter says she's pregnant and your first reaction is to put a bullet in her baby's daddy? How is that smart, Johnathan?"

"I didn't even realize I had pulled the gun," I replied defensively.

"Okay, but once you realized you had it out, you still didn't make a move to put it away. Your daughters are grown and they been living life while you were away, so don't start no bullshit with them now because they don't need it. Besides, are you trying to make your grandchild grow up without a father?"

Just the idea of me being a grandfather was staggering, let alone how that child would grow up. I knew Kamile was right, though, so I tucked my gun back into the waist of my slacks.

"Happy now?" I asked sarcastically.

"Yeah, but only because my nose has finally stopped bleeding. She got a mean left."

"Come here and let me see," I said, stepping closer to her.

Her nose was swollen and her eyes were a little puffy, but it didn't look like it was broken. Taking her face in my hands I turned it first left and then right confirming my earlier conclusion.

"You'll be a'ight."

"Nigga, you knew that before you took my face in your hands. You just wanted to perfectly position yourself to kiss me," she said confidently.

Instinctively, I was ready to argue and deny what she was saying, but I didn't see a point in that. So, I kissed her. Before my lips met hers, I'd had no idea if she would allow me to do what I was doing, but she opened her mouth to me and introduced our tongues in a way that had my heart racing.

One of my arms wrapped around her, pulling her firmly up against me, while my other hand slid under her short black dress in search of the panties that needed to come off. To my surprise, all I felt was smooth skin in the form of thick pussy lips that opened to me with the gentle nudge of my index finger. She was wetter than a Jacuzzi and twice as hot, which had my dick banging at my zipper like it wanted to fight.

"We ain't got much time. Get your finger out and put your dick in," she demanded.

I was already working on the zipper as I backed her up against the wall. And no sooner than I lifted her into the air, there came a knock at the door.

"Daddy?" Free called out.

It took everything in me not to shove my dick head inside Kamile, at least one time, but I saw the look on her face.

"It's gonna be too good to stop so we better not even start. Besides, I gotta go to work," she said, breathing heavily.

I was reluctant to let her down, but I did.

"Taste it," she said.

At first I was confused until she pulled my hand up in front of my face where I could see her juices running down my finger. Without a second thought, I put it in my mouth and savored her apple cinnamon taste.

"Dad, I need to talk to you," Free called again.

"Good, ain't it?" Kamile whispered, pulling me to her and kissing me once again.

I was just about to say fuck it when she backed up out of my reach and headed for the door.

"I'll be back later, or you can stop by the club if you feel the need," she said, opening the door and stepping past Free.

The two exchanged words, which gave me time to make sure I was decent, and I sat on the bed so the obvious wouldn't be seen.

"Dad, let me explain because-"

"You don't owe me any type of explanation. The news was just a shock, that's all. Why didn't you tell me?"

"Because you would've worried about me and I thought that would've made you risk your life by coming back. Why didn't you tell me you were still in the country?"

"Because you would've worried, and... damn, it sounds like we think alike, huh?" I asked, smiling.

"Of course, we do, I'm my father's daughter."

"Be careful how loud you say that, baby girl, you know a lot of people don't think too highly of your old man."

"Like I give a fuck what they think," she replied, sitting next to me on the bed.

"I know that, but you care what I think. And I think you and my grandbaby need to get somewhere safe."

"Dad, there's no place safer than with you," she said sincerely.

"I know you think that, but the feds ain't coming to ask me no questions or arrest me. They coming to knock my head off.

Angel's too, probably, now that she's out. You can't be nowhere around us if shit gets live. You know I'd never forgive myself if something happened. And from the looks of shit, neither would your baby daddy."

"Don't call him that. Bone is... he's everything. He's the man I love, the father of my child, my best friend, my right-hand man in the streets... he's everything."

"Sounds like you love him," I said.

"I do. Besides you, he's the realest nigga I ever met in my life. If you got to know him, I know you'd like him because real recognizes real."

I'd always considered Free to be a good judge of character because I'd instilled in her from a young age to be cynical, and believe that everybody wasn't shit. That way the good things you found in a person were bonuses because they were unexpected. I had no idea if dude was everything she said he was, but the least I could do was give him the benefit of doubt.

"If he is who you say he is, then he and I will agree that you can't be a part of this," I said.

"I'm stubborn enough to get my way against both of you. Plus, I've got a plan."

"Well the least I can do is hear you out," I conceded.

"I don't know if you noticed the high yellow chick hovering around Destiny, but that's our home girl, Black Sam, and she's the wizard with computers. The two big niggas who came in with me and Bone are brothers, Lil Boy and Big Baby, and murder is their expertise. Bone is the same way. All in all, that small crew out there in the living room is what has been controlling the streets of Atlanta with an iron fist while you were gone. We can handle Sapphire and the feds."

"Regardless of how you feel, Sapphire is still the woman who gave you life. I can't have you there when I take hers," I said, shaking my head.

"I can respect that. Anyway, the only way I can probably get Bone to agree to let me stay is if I'm ducked off in a house somewhere."

"So that's your plan?"

Oh, it'll be you, me, and Angel under house arrest, pops. Bone, Lil Boy, Big Baby, and Destiny ain't wanted, so when it's time to hit a location and put the press on a mufucka, they can handle that," she replied.

"Tell you what, I'ma wait to sell if you can see this idea to everybody else before I speak on it,"

"No problem, come on," she said, leading the way back into the living room.

All conversation ceased when we came in the room and Free commanded everyone's attention. Quickly she outlined the same plan she'd just run down to me. While she talked, I observed how everybody reacted.

It was clear that they were used to taking orders from Free, and the fact that they were even here meant their loyalty was unshakable. Despite the circumstances, I was proud of the women my daughters had become. There wasn't anything I'd change about them. After Free finished talking, nobody said anything, but Bone got up and went to Free's side.

"I'm not letting you out of my sight, you hear me?" he asked her.

The love she felt for him was evident, and I actually didn't mind because I knew she'd been taken care of when I was gone. That's important to any father.

"A'ight Freedom, you put this plan together, now organize it so it works. We need to move fast," I said.

# Chapter 12
## Freedom

One week later…

"I miss you, baby."

"I miss you, too. Why don't you let me see something?" he asked, smiling mischievously.

"What you wanna see with your nasty ass?" I asked playfully.

"You know what I want."

"Oh, boy you crazy as shit," I said, moving the laptop so he'd have a better angle, and pulling my wife beater up so he could see my barely bulging belly.

"That's what I'm talking about, that's sexy. Hey, little man, it's your daddy."

"Oh god, don't tell me you're gonna be one of those niggas who talks to my stomach during this whole pregnancy," I said, slightly distressed.

"You damn right, that's my first born in there and he need to know his pops is out here waiting on him."

"Okay, first of all, I'm barely three months pregnant, and secondly, how do you know it's a boy?" I asked, rolling my neck.

"Because the world can't handle another woman like you, and lord knows I can't," he replied laughing.

"You so stupid," I said, laughing with him.

One of the reasons I loved Bone so much was because when there was nothing in the world to be happy or smile about, he gave me a reason for both. From day one, life had been hectic, but my nigga was a soldier and that brought strength to our relationship.

"So how is everything?" I asked.

"I know this money is your first love, your first baby, but you should know we raised it right and it keeps growing even when we not around for the day to day grind."

"Good, so when will you be back?" I asked, hopeful now because it sounded like his business was complete.

All of us understood that our time was borrowed, so when we headed for the border, we needed to have as much money or more than the new government controlling whatever country we landed in. More money, more power was a universal theme.

"I'll be there within the next day or two, I just got a few loose ends to tie up. How's everything going on your end?" he asked.

"It's quiet. The crew is out doing some shopping right now because they're getting ready to take a trip."

"You not going, right?" he asked, giving me a look that was easy to interrupt because I'd made him a promise to stay out of the way.

"I'm not going anywhere, dad," I replied sarcastically.

"That's baby daddy, thank you very much."

"Oh, so you just my baby daddy now, nigga?" I asked, with a slight attitude.

"Don't get all emotional on me because you already know what it is. I love your crazy ass for better or for worse, and I know I proved that to you."

"Yes, you have, and you better love me because I'd hate to kill you."

"Damnnnn, you just gonna threaten me like that?" he asked, laughing.

"What you gonna do about it?"

"I'll show you when I get there, sweetheart."

"I'll be waiting on you. Go handle your business and get your ass back up here ASAP," I said, missing him more than I could say.

"I love you, and I'll see you soon."

"I love you, too," I replied, staring at the screen until he disappeared.

"Aww, you two are so cute."

"Fuck you, bitch, why you standing there eavesdropping?" I asked, slightly embarrassed.

"Because that's what little sisters do. Besides, my name is Angel, and since I am one I wouldn't consider what I was doing as eavesdropping, but more like using the gifts God gave me."

"More like Fathergod, you sneaky mufucka," I replied, laughing and throwing a pillow from the bed at her.

I wasn't really mad at her, it was just crazy that I hadn't noticed her standing in the bedroom doorway. Being that Kamile owned the building where my father had been staying, she gave us the three-bedroom basement apartment right next to his. It was tight with seven heads up in there, but most of the time Angel slept at dad's, and despite my objections, Destiny and Black Sam were shacked up, fucking like nymphos.

I wasn't mad, maybe a little jealous, though, because I wasn't getting no dick as long as Bone was in Atlanta securing the bag. I'd never understand how Angel could go without it.

"So, what's up, sis? What's on your mind?" I asked.

"Nothing. Why do you ask?"

"Well because your hair is a mess and you've got a comb in your hand. As I recall, that means you want me to braid your shit, and you wanna talk about something," I replied.

She didn't even try to hide the guilty smile as she came all the way into the room and sat on the floor in between my legs.

"What you want done?" I asked, taking the comb from her.

"Just give me some straight back cornrows."

That had been the ritual since we were kids. Whenever she or Destiny needed to talk, they'd get me to braid their hair. I don't know if it made them feel like they were at the salon where all women gossiped, or if it worked more like confessional where you didn't actually have to see the priest to receive absolution or feel comfort. Whatever the reason, I'd always been there, and I'd always be there as long as they needed me to be.

"So, what's up Angel, talk to me," I said, parting her hair and thus opening the confessional.

"I just been thinking. It seems like that's all I do anymore is think because I damn sure didn't think the night I ran up in that club. I was reckless and this got me and King Deuce fucked up."

"Shit happens, you know that's part of the game. You're out of that situation, though, and Miranda has already given KD's lawyer the greenlight to get himself out of that situation. Don't lose no sleep over that."

"It's not just that. I mean, life is different after you've tried to accept the fact that you're gonna die in prison. I didn't have to live with that reality as long as dad, but I understand a little better what he went through," she said, softly.

As close as I was to my father, that was a reality I didn't know, which meant for once I wasn't the person to help her deal with what she now felt.

"Have you talked to dad?" I asked.

"Yeah… but there's been other things on my mind that I can't go to him about."

"Such as?" I asked, more curious than worried.

"I've just been thinking about living life. I know that for some orphaned black kids from Atlanta, we've seen and done more than most, but there's still so much more to do. Once this is all over, I plan to get to it, but something else has been on my mind for the immediate future."

"Okay… well don't keep me in suspense, bitch," I said, laughing and giving her hair a little tug.

"That day in my cell, dude was gonna rape me. I saw the determination mixed with the madness in his eyes, Free. And my first thought was that this couldn't be the way I lost my virginity. I ain't scared of sex. I've just chosen to respect my body until the right man came along, but that decision was almost taken from me, and who knows how many times it would've happened after that. The reality that came from that situation is that nothing in life is promised, not tomorrow or the plans we make, nothing. So, we gotta live while we can."

"So, what are you saying, sweetie?" I asked seriously.

"I'm saying I wanna live… and I wanna know how it feels when somebody else knows my body. I might even want kids-"

"Whoa, slow down, bitch," I said, laughing.

"I'm not saying I'ma get pregnant now, Free. Damn, let me get the dick first and see if I like it. I might turn out to be like Destiny."

"Just because Destiny prefers women, don't get it twisted, she still will fall victim to some good dick," I assured her.

"How do you know when it's good?"

"Trust me, there won't be any mistake between identifying the good versus the bad. Good dick has a way of changing your views on life and what's important. It can be addictive if you're not careful, and it'll make you do some stupid shit."

"Damn, you make it sound like you can't control yourself," she replied, laughing nervously.

"Some women can't. Being dickmatized is a real thing, so my advice is to proceed with caution or you risk becoming a slave to that monster."

"I-I still want to know what it's about," she said, determined.

I'd always treated her as an adult who was capable of making her own decisions, but in that moment, I felt like a mother talking to her daughter, almost brought tears to my eyes.

"Well, I know you don't just wanna give it away to some random nigga so-"

"Actually, I have somebody in mind," she replied shyly.

"Who?" I asked, surprised at how fast this had developed.

"I'm saying, you know I could never fuck with a nigga I don't respect. I think Little Boy is a real nigga and-"

"Hold up, pause, you wanna fuck Little Boy? Have you even had a real conversation with him?" I asked, caught completely off guard by her choice.

"Yeah, bitch, you act like we just met for the first-time last week. You know we've known each other for years, and I always thought he was cute, but I wasn't ready to take it there."

"And now you ready to take it there? Yo, sis, I ain't trying to be funny, but have you seen that niggas dick?" I asked, laughing.

"You so stupid, why would you ask me some shit like that?"

"Because he's working with a monster, real life. I don't think your first time should be with a nigga packing like that, but that's just my opinion," I said.

"Does it hurt that bad?"

If the niggas who throw money at her and watched her dance could hear this shy girl sitting in between my legs, they wouldn't believe it. I actually felt honored that she could be this vulnerable with me because I knew she wasn't like that with the world.

"I mean, the first time you're gonna feel discomfort. The trick is to make sure your dude knows it's your first time so he can be gentle, and so he can prepare himself."

"Prepare himself? For what?" she asked.

"Because a tight pussy is a man's kryptonite. Once he's in it, he can rarely control himself, and he'll be trying to knock your uterus out."

"Oh… well I think Little Boy would be gentle," she said, confidently.

"Even if he was gentle, a dick that size for your first time is suicide, sis. Let me ask you something though… knowing what almost happened to you in jail, how do you see Lil Boy? I know you remember what happened at that warden's house with his wife."

"Yeah, I remember… but I know why he did what he did. I'm not making excuses, but I'm not being hypocritical either because he did what he did for us and our family. I never want to be on the other end of that, but it doesn't make me see him no different," she replied.

"Okay. You're a grown woman, Angel, and I trust your judgement as much as I trust you. So whatever decision you make, I support you."

"Thanks, sis, I love-"

"Free, I think I got something," Black Sam announced, hurrying into the room with her laptop in hand.

"What you got?" I asked, stopping in the middle of braiding so she would have my undivided attention.

"I finally got into the federal files pertaining to the BGFF RICO case and those indictments are signed and sealed, which means they'll be delivered at any time. I didn't find Sapphire's name anywhere in the paperwork, but there is a confidential informant named Jewel Sky."

"You think that's my mother?" I asked.

"She seems to be the lynch pin to their case against her boyfriend, a nigga named Tony Mack, who is allegedly slinging dope across the Midwest and out to the west coast."

"I'll ask my dad if he knows dude or his chick. Did they have any info on Jewel Sky?"

"No, just that she's one of many who helped make their case, but she is the only female informant listed," Black Sam said, smiling.

"It's gotta be her then," Angel said, looking up at me.

"Yeah, but we still don't know where to find her snitchin' ass," I reminded her.

"But we do know where to find the lady who drafted the indictments," Black Sam said, hitting keys on her laptop until she got the screen she wanted so she could show me what she found.

"Ursula Inman, and what do we know about Ms. Inman?" I asked.

"She's from the south side of Chicago, single mother of two, a boy that's eight and a girl that's six. She thirty-four years old, black, and lives with her elderly mother. She's been working for the US Attorney's office for about four years."

"Have Destiny and the guys come back yet?" I asked.

"No."

"Angel, where's dad?"

"He was asleep when I came over here. You know he hasn't been doing much of that lately," she replied.

Looking up in the corner of Sam's computer screen, I saw it was just after 6pm, which meant Ursula should be at home with the kids. There was a voice in my mind telling me not to think what I was thinking, but louder than that voice was the sound of opportunity knocking. That wasn't something I could ignore.

"Angel, hit Kamile and tell her we need a ride, no questions. We got work to do."

# Chapter 13
### Destiny

"Can you niggas explain to me why we had to go way to fucking St. Louis to get the shit we needed?"

"Sure, I'll let Big Baby tell you," Lil Boy said, laughing.

"Very funny asshole, but the day that nigga does speak, I guarantee he cusses your ass out first for all of your bullshit," I replied, laughing when Big Baby turned towards me and shook his head in agreement.

I never understood what it was that prevented him from talking, but I was smart enough to know it would be insensitive to make that a topic of conversation. Regardless of whatever, that was my nigga, and we went back to the days at the roller-skating rink when I used to sell weed for Free. He had my back and I had his, no words could change that.

"I'm serious, though, with all the shootings in Chicago, I know we could've picked up some guns without having to go out of town," I said.

"Yeah, we probably could've, but my nigga I know you dead ass tired of being cooped up in that apartment. I don't care how good Black Sam pussy is, you still like fresh air, too,'" Lil Boy reasoned.

I couldn't deny the truth in what he said because sometimes it felt like the walls were trying to close in. It had been good to take a road trip, especially since Big Baby had been behind the wheel of the black 2015 Expedition the entire time. I was riding shot gun, but I still felt like I was being chauffeured.

"Tell me this, though, bruh, what the hell type of gun is a LARS 47?" I asked.

"It's like a chopper and an R-15 all in one, and it shoots chopper bullets. I'm telling you it's a bad mufucka. You should've got you one."

"My nigga, that may be a bad piece, but that Chrome Uzi in the trunk ain't no bitch and it ain't playing no games. You already know I'm on one," I said, laughing.

One thing I knew for sure was that whenever we get down to the action, we were gonna ring bells like school was out.

"What I really wanna know is how did you get a gun connect in St. Louis that even I didn't know about?" I asked, turning around in my seat to face Lil Boy.

"I been known to make a move here and there. I just keep my ears open and pick up the seeds the others drop. I learned that from you."

"I can dig that. I guess I'm surprised we actually paid for some shit instead of getting it how we live," I said, turning back around.

Robbing mufuckas was what we did best, and truthfully, it was the most fun crime to commit in my opinion. Taking something from someone who took it from somebody else was how the food chain worked, and Free had always taught us to be the most ruthless animal in the jungle. This was one of those situations where doing straight business just seemed weird to me, but Lil Boy had set it up, so I rolled with it.

"I'm hungry as shit. We need to… hold that thought," I said, reaching for the ringing phone in my jeans pocket.

"Hey you," I said.

"H-hey. Listen, I think I fucked up and you're gonna be mad, but I didn't mean to and-"

"Whoa, slow down, Samantha, and tell me what the problem is."

"Okay. I found some information about that thing I've been working on for you know who. I thought it was better to take it to Free first and run it down to her, and I thought she would run it past you all."

"But?" I prompted. Getting a bad feeling in the pit of my stomach about where this was going.

"But she said it was something light and could be handled in no time. That was an hour ago, and now I'm worried."

"Who's with her?" I asked, signaling Big Baby with my hand to drive this mufucka faster.

"Well you know who is sleeping so she only had her Guardian Angel by her side."

Both of my sisters were more than capable, and the fact that Free was pregnant didn't lessen her abilities in the slightest. Even knowing that, I couldn't stop the worry that flooded my blood stream and had my heart pounding harder, or how suddenly dry my mouth was. I'd never questioned Free's judgement, but right about now I was feeling like this bitch done lost her mind.

"Send the address to my phone," I ordered.

"It should be coming through now. Destiny, please don't be mad at me. I didn't know-"

"I'm not mad. Whatever you do, though, don't say shit to you know who because that'll only end badly. Stay in the house, in the bedroom, and wait on my call," I said, hanging up.

"What's going on?" Lil Boy asked.

"Free got a lead and she took Angel with her to handle it."

Hearing this revelation Big Baby put the petal to the floor, demanding all the horse power that Ford had to offer.

"Where's your dad?"

"He's sleep, and I know Bone is still in Atlanta," I replied, pulling up the address Black Sam had sent.

Quickly I punched it into the trucks GPS so Big Baby would know where we were going. Luckily, we were only thirty minutes away.

"Get my gun out the back," I told Lil Boy, knowing that we had to show up on the scene ready for absolutely whatever.

I wanted to text Black Sam and ask her who the target had been, but there was only so much information I was willing to exchange over a phone, even a clean one. Instead I sent her a text telling her to hit me up immediately if they came home.

"Here," Lil Boy said, handing me the duffel bag with my Uzi, three magazines, and a couple boxes of bullets.

I could hear him behind me starting to load up his LARS .47 and I followed suit. Luckily for Big Baby, his preference was the .50 Cal. Desert Eagle sitting in his lap, and it was already loaded for war so all he had to do was drive. That task suddenly became more difficult when we re-entered Chicago because there were red and blue lights flashing behind us.

"You gotta be fucking kidding me," I growled through clenched teeth.

Big baby looked over at me and I could see the question in his eyes. Did I want him to pull over? Fuck nah. But we both knew that he couldn't outrun the cops in this big ass truck. Reluctantly, I tucked my gun back into the duffel bag and put it on the floor in front of me.

"Everybody tuck your shit. Go ahead and pull over, bruh," I said, hoping we could get through a routine traffic stop.

He made a right onto a side street and came to a stop, pulling his shirt down over the pistol, but now moving it from his lap. The truck was legal, although the tint was probably past the limits allowed. Speed had to be the reason we were getting pulled over so hopefully it would be a quick ticket and we could be on our way.

"Why ain't nobody stepped out the car yet?" Lil Boy asked, after we'd been sitting there for almost five minutes.

"I don't know, but just be cool," I replied, checking the side and rearview mirrors as nonchalantly as I could.

In response to my statement, I heard Lil Boy force a clip into his gun and pull the slide back to put that first bullet on the VIP list for the party. I didn't wanna think he had the right idea, but the longer we sat, the more uneasy I felt. After another two minutes passed, my uneasiness was rewarded because another cop car pulled up behind the first.

"Aw shit. Lil Boy, keep that thing out of sight. We got four cops walking up on us."

"Four cops? That means we're outnumbered and we're riding dirty? Man, fuck that," he replied, turning around in his seat and turning the back glass into crushed glass when he squeezed the trigger.

The two cops approaching my side of the car fell immediately, but the other two ran back to their cars for cover. I could tell Big Baby was getting ready to mash off, but we couldn't leave any witnesses, especially cops.

"Hold on, Big Baby," I said, scrambling for the bag at my feet and grabbing the Uzi out of it. It would've been easier to hop out of the truck and slaughter them, but I could still see people on the street and we didn't need witnesses identifying us.

"Back up so we can get 'em," I ordered, climbing into the back seat with Lil Boy in time to empty clips into the second car.

Once we saw the other cops' bodies drop, Big Baby threw the truck in drive and got us the hell out of there with the quickness.

"Why the fuck did you start shooting?" I yelled at Lil Boy.

"Because them mufuckas was definitely gonna pull our black asses out this truck. What you think happens next? Stop acting like cops don't kill mufuckas for less. And this is Chiraq. We got way too much fire power in this bitch to act like we out for a Sunday drive."

I knew he was right about everything he said so there was really no point in me arguing with him. In any other circumstance, I probably would've been the first mufucka to shoot, but my primary concern right now was not bringing unwanted attention to any of us. Knocking off four cops was certainly the opposite of that.

"Big Baby, get us to that address ASAP because we gotta get my sisters and prepare to get the fuck out of dodge."

"What we need to do is dump this truck," Lil Boy said, looking behind us to see who was following us.

Again, he was right, but I damn sure didn't wanna get rid of it if I couldn't destroy it because our prints and DNA were all over it.

"Pull up at this corner store right here," I said, passing my gun to Lil Boy.

"What you-"

The rest of his question was tossed to the wind because I was already out the truck and jogging to the store. Once I was inside, I found their liquor section and grabbed a couple bottles of Rum and Vodka. When I got to the counter, I dropped a $50 dollar bill, grabbed two lighters, and I was back out the door headed for the truck.

"What the hell are you doing?" Lil Boy asked, since I was back inside.

"Molotov cocktails… start ripping off pieces of your shirt, Big Baby get us to the nearest projects," I ordered as I opened the first bottle of liquor and poured it all over the interior of the truck.

It wasn't dynamite or a grenade, but it would get the job done. Grabbing my gun and Lil Boy's, I stuffed them inside the duffel bag and made sure we weren't leaving anything important or identifiable behind. A couple minutes later, we pulled over into a rundown neighborhood, where more than likely even if the cops were called they wouldn't respond.

Once we had the remaining three bottles rigged, we hopped out and I lit the first fuse, tossing it on the floor. I handed one bottle and a lighter to Lil Boy, he lit his as I did mine and we threw them through the trucks windows, immediately sending it up in flames.

"Big Baby, we need a ride," I said, shouldering the duffel bag as we set off down the street.

I had no idea where the fuck we were, but I felt exposed being out there on the street knowing what we'd gotten ourselves into. As if on cue, a white old school Cutlass turned the corner and was creeping in our direction. Big Baby stepped in the middle of the street, forcing the car to stop, and then he pulled his gun. Through the windshield, I could see two kids in car seats, and they looked like miniature versions of the woman driving.

"Not them," I said, passing the duffel bag to Lil Boy and instructing him and his brother to let me handle the problem of our transportation.

We walked on for another block and a half before I spotted a money green Denali coming towards us. Even though I only had on some stone washed jeans, a white t-shirt, and blue and white Jordan's, I knew I could still get a niggas attention. I didn't walk in the middle of the street, but close enough that all the driver had to do was stop to exchange words with me. And that's exactly what he did.

"How you doing, sweetheart?" he asked.

"I'm good, how about you?" I replied, taking in the diamonds in both his earrings and chain, his handsome face, and his lack of passengers all in one quick glance.

"You know you too fine to be out here walking, especially in this neighborhood. Come on, let me give you a ride."

"You gonna take me where I wanna go?" I asked, feigning innocence and slight seduction all at the same time.

"Of course, all you gotta do is hop in the truck."

I didn't say a word, I simply strutted around the front of his truck to the passenger door, knowing he'd be watching my ass, and not Big Baby. By the time I got to the passenger door and opened it, Big Baby had that .50 at his head, pulling him out the truck.

"Don't worry about the truck, just be grateful you keeping your life," I said, nodding at Big Baby to let him go.

Dude was smart enough to run away and not look back either. We quickly piled into the truck and took off, needing to put distance between us and everything that had gone wrong in the last twenty minutes. I pulled out my phone to get the address to type into the truck's GPS only to find a text from Black Sam saying I needed to get back to the apartment ASAP. Once I had that address typed into the system, Big Baby navigated the streets with a purpose, getting us back to safety in thirty minutes and without having to kill nobody.

"That shit was crazy," I said, getting out of the truck and going to the elevator.

"Hell yeah, but we make too good a team to get caught up, no matter what streets we in," Lil Boy replied, smiling with relief.

It wasn't until we were in the elevator on the way down that I caught the look Big Baby was giving me.

"I know, we gotta lay low," I said, disappointed that we'd brought heat to an already flaming situation.

Laying low might not be enough, we might have to get out of town ahead of schedule because I doubted Chicago PD was gonna stand for four of their people getting killed. Just one more thing I was gonna have to discuss with my father in the near future.

"What the fuck is this?" I asked, coming through the door to find a bitch butt naked and spread eagle on the living room floor.

"Get in here," Free ordered, standing over the obviously unconscious woman.

I knew that look on Free's face. I'd seen it a time or two, and we referred to it as beast mode. The light of the intelligence and comprehension was clear and bright in her eyes, but you couldn't find an ounce of compassion or empathy. The animal in her had taken over, and everybody knew what happened when the lion was lose. Whoever this woman was, she was on borrowed time.

Aryanna

# Chapter 14
## Angel

As I sat and watched Free loom over the naked, helpless woman I wondered how a simple job of going to get answers had turned into kidnapping. When we'd left to go have a chat with Ursula, that's all it was supposed to have been. I mean, she had too much to lose not to give us the information we wanted, right? Well somehow between the ride to her house and finding her not far from the location walking her dog, things changed.

On short notice, the only ride Kamile had been able to get was a dark blue Dodge Caravan, but it had served its purpose of being inconspicuous and non-threatening in Ursula's middle class neighborhood. Plus, Free's added request of a Glock .17, made it all too easy to force a woman off the street without drawing attention to ourselves. The problem was the bitch thought we were playing.

After a few minutes of trying to reason with her, and even bribe her, Free simply smacked her across the head with the pistol and put her to sleep. After that, she wasn't a problem, but our problem was we needed a spot to take her where the interrogation could be handled. I thought we should've just called Kamile since we were in her city and she was bound to have different places we could use, but Free didn't want Kamile to know what we were up to because she thought it would get back to dad.

Ordinarily, I would've said she was trippin', and she was crazy for keeping shit from dad, but it was obvious something was going on between him and Kamile. So, after a brief moment of not knowing what the hell we were gonna do, we'd decided to bring Ursula back to the apartment, not the brightest idea, but neither was riding around the city with a bitch unconscious on the floor.

"Free, who the fuck is that?" Destiny asked, once the door had closed behind her, Big Baby, and Lil Boy.

I knew the look on Frees face meant she was intensely focused on what had to be done, so explaining herself wasn't a priority. I quickly explained to Destiny who Ursula Inman was and what had happened, but I could tell she was only listening with half an ear. She had something on her mind as well.

"So, what's the plan, Free?" Destiny asked.

"I need a power drill."

"A power drill?" I asked, confused by her choice of weapon.

"Yeah, a power drill and a hammer. One of you go find the maintenance man for this building and get it done," she ordered, never taking her eyes off the naked woman at her feet,

"I got it," Lil Boy volunteered, passing Destiny a duffel bag and going back out the front door.

Each of us had learned in the street that you did whatever had to be done to succeed at the task at hand, but sometimes Free could get on some next level shit. This was starting to look like one of those times.

"Are you sure this bitch knows where Sapphire is?" Destiny asked.

"I don't know what she knows, but I'ma find out. Grab a chair and strap her to it, and make sure you gag her so she can't scream," Free said dispassionately.

Big Baby moved to complete the tasks and Destiny joined me on the couch.

"She's on one," Destiny whispered to me.

"I know, but I think it's because she wants this shit to be over so we can leave and get a fresh start," I replied softly.

"We might gotta leave sooner than later."

"What the fuck does that mean, Destiny, what happened?" I asked, wondering what else could go wrong today.

After she ran down the details of the little trip she'd just taken, I understood a lot could go wrong in a day. I damn sure didn't wanna be the one responsible for updating my father because he was definitely gonna feel some type of way. While Destiny got up to go holler at Black Sam, I watched Ursula being secured to a chair with zip ties. She still wasn't conscious, but she damn sure wouldn't be going anywhere in the near future.

She appeared to be nothing more than a slightly overweight, aging black woman, with plenty of gray in her hair, but she'd have to be some type of warrior to keep information away from Free.

Within five minutes, Lil Boy came back through the door carrying a small green bag, which he passed to Free.

"You need anything else?" he asked.

"Some plastic, this could be messy," Free replied, inspecting the contents of the bag.

As Lil Boy journeyed off again in search of the needed material, my mind flashed back to the conversation Free and I had had not long ago. It wasn't Lil Boy's smooth chocolate skin or his sometimes-lazy smile, or even his light brown eyes that made him sexy to me. He was loyal, and in a high-pressure situation, he wouldn't bend or fold. He was a man despite his name. I could admit that now wasn't the time to be thinking about getting some dick, but watching him in action always made me feel some type of way.

"Did you hear me, Angel?" Free asked.

"Huh?"

"I said I want you to start with her feet," she repeated.

I'd been so far off in my own world that I hadn't seen the metal hammer she was holding out to me. I took it and moved over to the bound and gagged woman, kneeling right next to her.

"Wake her up," Free said.

Taking careful aim, I cocked the hammer and brought it down with determined force on the big toe of her right foot, feeling the bone shatter like a champagne glass at a Jewish wedding. Instantly, Ursula was back from the land of slumber and this was evidenced by her muffled screams and the piss that damn near got on me.

"You can scream all you'd like, but ain't no savior coming. And since you wanted to be so fucking hard headed, I'm not gonna ask you a question until every toe on that foot is broken," Free said calmly.

The woman's screams were accompanied by tears now, and she was still pissing, which made me back up a little because it had my eyes burning.

"I'm telling you now that if you shit I'm shove this hammer up your funky ass, and the handle won't be going first," I warned.

"Next toe," Free ordered.

I could see the pleading in her eyes, but there was no compassion in mine because we'd tried to do shit the easy way first. Kneeling beside her again, I swung the hammer swiftly and crushed two toes for the price of one causing her to scream in agony all over again.

True to her word, Free stood right next to the screaming woman and didn't ask her shit, although it was clear to see Ursula now wanted to say something. The front door opened again and Lil Boy came in carrying a blue tarp.

"Will this work?" he asked.

"Yeah, and we need it because this bitch already pissed herself," I replied, moving out of his way.

"Damn you just started," he said, nodding at his brother to pick Ursula up so he could unroll the tarp.

"Angel let me see that hammer," Free said.

I passed it to her, wondering if she was about to get in on part of the action, but instead she took the drill bit for the power drill and knelt down on a corner of the tarp. I was confused about what she was doing until I saw her use the hammer to break the rounded part of the bit off, leaving jagged metal edges on all sides. Ursula was in too much pain to watch, but I was paying attention and this definitely wasn't gonna end well for her.

"Finish that foot," Free instructed, passing me the hammer back once Big Baby sat the chair with the screaming woman down on the tarp.

I smashed her last two toes and moved on to pulverizing the rest of the bones in her foot with repeated swings. Suddenly, the screaming stopped and I looked up to see that Ursula was again unconscious.

"My bad, sis," I said.

"No worries, I know what'll wake her up," she replied, putting the bit back in the drill and testing it to make sure it worked.

In that moment, she looked like some deranged serial killer from a 90's movie. My first thought was that she was gonna drill all types of holes in Ursula Inman, but when she put the drill up to her ear and slowly wedged it inside I knew this was about to get interesting. The drill bit was at least 7 inches long which meant it wouldn't take much pushing to scramble ole girl's brains like Sunday morning eggs.

"Lil Boy, get a pot of cold water," Free said.

He quickly disappeared into the kitchen and returned moments later with what she requested. Once Free had taken the tool out of Ursula's ear and stepped back, Lil Boy tossed the water on her, causing her to wake up and re-enter her world of pain.

"You don't get to sleep, bitch. Now comes the question and answer portion of the program. I know you see this drill in my hand, but I want you to pay close attention to the tip and how sharp the edges are. Hold her head Big Baby," Free instructed.

Naturally Ursula struggled, but there were no illusions about whether or not the end result would be the same. Once Free had the drill back in her ear, though, she was smart enough to go perfectly still.

"Listen to me very carefully, Ursula, because I'm only gonna say this once. Jewel Sky," Free said slowly before untying the gag from her mouth,

"Sh-sh-she's a witness, an in-informant in a RICO case."

"Skip to the parts we don't know, like where is she," I said.

"S-safe house until trial, in-in-in Gary, Indiana, but sh-she'll be moving s-soon the indictments will be out."

"When?" Free asked,

"I-I don't kn-know."

"Ursula," Free said in a sing song kinda way.

"I sw-swear to God, I don't know," she replied, empathetically, crying harder as Free slowly moved the drill in and out of her ear, almost like she was fucking her.

Maybe mind fucking her was a more accurate description.

"When you drafted the indictments, I'm pretty sure you had to let someone know that they were ready, and official paperwork had to be done for subpoenas. Jewel Sky would've had to get one, so who delivers it Ursula?" Free asked.

"N-no subpoena, she's a cooperating w-witness. Only the special-special agent in charge of the Chicago FBI f-field office knows where sh-she is."

"And his name is?" I asked, raising the hammer in a threatening way.

"Michael Needham," she blurted, flinching, but unable to move because of the restraints and the tool in her ear.

"Black Sam," I hollered, sitting the hammer down and moving to the couch.

Moments later she appeared with Destiny in tow, and I could tell by their body language that whatever conversation they'd been having was heated.

"We need all the information you can get on a guy named Michael Needham, he's a special agent in charge for the Chicago branch of the FBI," I said.

"Is there anything else you wanna tell us, Ursula, it might save your life?" Free said sweetly.

"I-I have k-kids, please-"

"You're dealing with people who ain't very empathetic or understanding, so that declaration does you no good," Free whispered in her ear, pushing the drill bit in further.

"H-hotel! When they b-bring Jewel here, they'll stash her in a hotel, and there's only three that we use. I know which ones they are."

"The names?" I asked, pulling my phone out so I could text them to myself.

"How do I know y-you'll let me go once I've helped you?" Ursula asked.

"How do you know we won't send someone to go pick up your kids or your mom?" Free countered.

In that moment, I saw Ursula crumble because the harsh reality was that she had no bargaining chips with us. No one did, and the reason for this was because civilized society had limitations to what they would and wouldn't do. Aside from Ursula and maybe Black Sam no one else in this room suffered from that affliction. We did whatever, whenever, to whoever with little to no regard, and remorse wasn't a word in our vocabulary.

"Your call Ursula," I said patiently.

Her tears rained harder as she gave me the listing of the three hotels along with what assumed names or corporations might be used to check in, depending on how many witnesses would be there at once.

"Now Ursula I want you to hold still because if you move, I might accidently-"

Suddenly, the power drill came to life in Free's hand, and even though Ursula screamed, it was cut short as its pinnacle when Free shoved the tool through her eardrum into her brain. I'd anticipated the whole scene being a lot messier, but aside from the blood now trickling from her nose and ear, she appeared to be sleeping,

"A'ight, we got information to go on, so let's find this bitch and get out of dodge," Free said, wiping her prints off the power drill and dropping it back in the bag.

Big Baby started cutting the restraints off of her body and removed her from the chair so he could roll her up in the tarp. Everybody was moving and getting ready for the next step, except for Destiny and Black Sam.

"What's going on with you two? Now ain't the time for a lover's quarrel, we got shit to do," I said seriously.

They exchanged a look between each other that I didn't understand, but something was definitely wrong.

"Free, we got a problem," Destiny finally said.

Everyone stopped what they were doing and turned to her.

"Some shit popped off on our way back from St. Louis and some cops got killed. I didn't get out the truck, but according to the research Black Sam just did, there are some picture's that'll hit the ten o'clock news. I know we're close to finishing this thing, but if the feds figure out it's me, they're gonna bring all of Chicago law enforcement down on us. They're gonna hunt all of us. Free, we got no choice, we gotta run."

# Chapter 15
## Fathergod

"Well this is a surprise. I definitely wasn't expecting to see you this early. Did you close the club?"

"Very funny, Johnathan, is that your way of saying I'm a workaholic?"

"You know you're a workaholic," I replied, laughing and stepping aside so she could enter the apartment.

"Hard work pays off, and besides, no one can do my job better than me. I do, however, have competent employees so the club is open for the happy hour crowd."

"So what's so important that you would step away from your money machine and visit little ole me?" I asked, pouring us both a drink from the bottle of Hennessey that had become a permanent fixture on my coffee table.

"Just checking on you, I mean, I know you don't get out much and with everyone up here you've been focused on keeping a low profile," she replied, accepting her drink and taking a seat on the couch,

"Yeah, but hopefully this shit will be over soon."

"Sounds like you ready to move on with life," she commented.

"Hell yeah. I mean, I just spent a decade in prison for a crime I was only partially guilty of. In reality, what I'd done could be perceived as self-defense since the nigga came to my house intending to body me, but the system don't give a fuck about right and wrong, or justice. A nigga's life is always expendable."

"So, what are you planning to do with the rest of your life?"

I gave her question careful consideration while sitting next to her on the couch. It was a question I'd asked myself from time to time over the years during those rare moments I envisioned another reality besides dying in prison. The answer was simple though.

"I'ma live."

"And what exactly does that mean?" she asked.

"I don't know, but whatever I do, I'ma do it with no regrets because every day of my life is borrowed time. I gotta make it count."

My response put a somewhat confused look on her face, but it didn't take away from her beauty. I was too much of a gangsta to tell her that she'd been on my mind since our encounter in the bedroom, but she had been. Truthfully, with her sitting here in that form fitting blue dress that just barely reached her knees, I wanted to pull her close, and find out if she had panties on.

"Why you looking at me like that?" I asked.

"I don't know, I guess I just didn't expect your answer to be so simple, but yet so deep. I ain't never had to do a bid, but I know it changes you. I know you're very ruthless, but it also seems like you've found a way to harness the shit until it's time not to anymore."

"It's called calculation," I replied.

"I'm aware, and I'm also a very calculating person."

"Oh yeah, how so?" I asked, intrigued by her.

"I felt our physical attraction from the jump, but I wasn't sure it was a smart idea. Plus, I've never felt it with such intensity on both parts. I had to evaluate and decide how best to proceed."

"Oh really, and what did you come up with?"

"Wipe that damn smile off your face, Johnathan, because you know what I came up with. You gonna get some of this pussy, but on my terms," she replied calmly.

It took effort on my part, but somehow, I managed to keep a straight face for my next question.

"What are your terms?"

"Well, I could tell you," she said, tossing her shot back and setting her glass on the table, before standing up and grabbing her purse. "Or I could show you," she teased, heading in the direction of my bedroom.

Finishing my own shot, I played it cool on the outside, but inside I was anticipating knocking the walls loose on that pussy. Taking my time, I followed in the direction she'd gone. When I got to my room, I found her standing next to the bed wearing nothing except the blue suede pumps she'd walked in on. Never had I ever doubted her beauty, but to see her naked proved to me how much clothes really concealed.

There wasn't an ounce of fat on her body and her skin looked so soft that I thought it might bruise under my touch. On top of that, I couldn't remember the last time I saw titties so firm.

"I'll take the fact that your mouth is hanging open as a compliment," she said, smiling.

I tried to play off the fact that I was embarrassed about being caught damn near drooling by advancing on her with thoughts of sexual destruction on my mind.

"Not so fast," she said, holding her hand up. "My terms, remember?"

"Okay. I'm following your lead," I replied, putting my hands up in surrender.

"Now you're understanding. Take off all your clothes," she demanded.

Years spent lifting weights to pass time had made my body a work of art, so I was all too happy to display it for her. I didn't waste no time with a strip tease, I got naked in a hurry. Her eyes appraised me in a slow measured way that was arousing for both of us. But instead of moving towards the hunger I saw in her, I waited for instruction.

"Lay on the bed, and don't think about having an opinion about what happens next," she said, picking her purse up off the floor.

I did what she said, watching her as she reached inside her purse and came out with several different silk scarves, I opened my mouth to say something, but the look she gave me said I needed to shut the fuck up and enjoy the moment. In all my years, I'd never experimented with bondage, but I guess the plus to this was that she'd been smart enough not to bring handcuffs to this party. That might've gotten her fucked up. It took her ten minutes to secure my hands and feet to the bed, and with every limb that was forced into limited mobility, I felt more and more vulnerable. This wasn't the feeling I was used to, or one that I liked.

"Kamile listen-"

"No talking, Johnathan. Don't worry, you're safe with me," she purred, running her finger nails lightly down my chest until she came to my dick.

The way she touched me made me feel like it was the first time a woman had ever touched me before, and all I could do was pray I didn't cum quick.

"Why you shaking, Johnathan, you nervous?"

"Fuck you," I replied through clenched teeth, fighting to control my breathing as she ran her hand up and down my shaft slowly.

"Oh, you will, that I can promise," she replied, smiling.

If I'd thought her hand was dangerous, I was in no way prepared for her mouth. Laying there helplessly, I watched as her succulent lips wrapped around my dick head like it was the worlds sweetest lollipop, and she sucked it so gently. Slowly she made me disappear down her throat until I could see her lips dancing with my pubic hair, while all nine inches of me was being introduced to her tonsils. She didn't gag, she didn't flinch, and throughout this entire experience, she'd been staring me directly in the eyes.

I was so turned on my dick hurt. As she slowly began the journey back up to only having the head in her mouth. I had to force myself not to cum because I didn't ever want this to end, but I need not have worried because she took it all the way out of her mouth.

"I can tell by your breathing and how hard your dick started throbbing in the back of my throat that you can't handle the head game yet. That's okay, we'll get there," she said, standing up on the bed and giving me an amazing view of her pretty pussy.

I didn't trust my voice not to crack so I didn't even try to use it.

"You think you ready for this?" she asked.

My response was to nod my head, which was her cue. Without hesitation, she straddled me, but she took me inside her as slowly and deliberately as she'd done with her mouth. I'd never felt a pussy so tight, wet, or hot in all my life, and by the time I was submerged inside her, I was pinned to the bed in fear.

"I can see it in your eyes," she whispered, "Don't be scared of the pussy."

And with that being said, she began to ride me. I wanted to touch her so fucking bad, but knowing that I couldn't kinda turned me on even more. She put her hands on my chest to give her that leverage she needed to go straight up and down. Once she got going, she was an absolute fool on my dick.

"I know it's g-good to you. I can see y-you fighting not to c-c-cum," she panted, speeding up a little, rising higher so she could fall faster.

Even if I wanted to respond, I couldn't.

"Oh-oh shit! Mmm-mmph! I'm 'bout to-I'm-I'm-"

I knew exactly what she was trying to say because I could feel her tightening her pussy in anticipation and I was right there with her, but suddenly she stopped.

"Wh-what are you doing?" I asked, trying to catch my breath.

"It's called edging. It's when you get to the point where you're about to cum, but you stop so you don't."

"But-"

"My terms," she replied, slapping me across the face.

For the first time, I actually tested the strength of my bindings, but luckily for her, they held.

"I see the fight in you, and that's good. Now fuck me," she demanded, slapping me a little harder.

For the next hour, we battled in a way that I never had before. With her on top of me I bucked as hard as I could, loving how her eyes rolled into the back of her head when I hit that sweet spot. At times, I thought I would die if she didn't let me cum, but the pussy was so good that I wanted to stay in it forever.

"Whose dick is this?"

At first I thought I didn't hear the question right, but she rode me harder, digging her nails into my chest.

"Whose-dick-is-this?" she growled through clenched teeth, her hazel eyes blazing hungrily down at me.

I was scrambling to hold on, but still I didn't answer.

"You c-can't fight it, Johnathan, this p-p-pussy is too good. I know you wanna c-cum. Whose-whose dick is it?" she asked, riding me like I'd never been rode before.

"It's yours, yours," I mumbled weakly, cumming so hard I thought I was gonna black out. I felt her cum with me right before she collapsed on my chest. I wanted to hold her close, but instead I had to settle for her holding me.

I closed my eyes for just a second, but the next thing I knew I heard insistent knocking coming from the front door. I thought it had only been a second, but the shadows in the room were different and Kamile was asleep on my chest. When the knocking came again, she stirred slightly.

"Kamile, baby, wake up, somebody's at the door."

Instantly, she came awake and I could see the question in her eyes was the same one I was thinking. Who the fuck would be knocking at my door? She hopped up and went straight for her purse coming out with a Chrome .44 and a straight razor. Swiftly she cut my right hand free and gave me the razor while she put on the t-shirt I'd discarded and headed out into the living room, pistol at ready. Quickly pulling on some basketball shorts, I grabbed the MAC-12 I kept under the bed and followed her.

Neither of us stood directly in front of the door as we listened to see what we could hear.

"Who is it?" I called.

"Daddy, it's us," came the reply.

When Kamile pulled the door open, there stood my three daughters, and the look on their faces meant they weren't bringing good news.

"Why the fuck is y'all knocking on the door like the feds?" I asked, irritated.

"I didn't take the key with me and I accidentally locked the door," Angel replied sheepishly.

"I'm going to get dressed," Kamile said, heading for the bedroom.

A big part of me wanted to go with her, but it was obvious my daughters had something on their mind, especially since there hadn't been any comments or sideways looks about Kamile.

"No dramatic shit or long drawn out explanations, just tell me what the problem is," I said, going to the couch and taking a seat.

One by one they filed in, closing the door and taking a seat across from me. All three wore different expressions on their faces, which undoubtedly meant that there was a difference of opinion somewhere in whatever the conflict was.

"Angel and Destiny gotta leave because-"

"We all gotta leave, Free," Destiny said, with both reluctance and anger.

"I'm not the one who fucked up so-"

"Neither am I, but shit happens sometime. We were outnumbered-"

"Will you two stop fucking arguing and make some sense out of this shit? Matter fact, you two don't say shit else. Angel, you tell me what's going on," I demanded impatiently, sitting my gun beside me on the couch and fixing myself a drink.

At first Angel was hesitant, but finally she began to explain everything that had happened on what I'd considered to be a good day, up to that point. Listening to her tell me about the decisions and moves that had been made, and the subsequent fall out, made me trade my shot glass for the full bottle because I definitely needed a drink.

I loved my children dearly and I knew they moved with the best of intentions, but goddammit they were hard headed. And now there was even more scrutiny and attention that we didn't need coming our way. For a full five minutes after Angel had finished speaking, I didn't say a word. I simply stared at them and took healthy gulps from my Hennessey bottle. I needed to compose myself because if I opened my mouth to speak I'd probably start screaming at them like a crazy person, only because they deserved it.

"Kamile," I yelled, summoning her from the bedroom, where she'd stayed to give us some privacy.

"Yes, Johnathan?" she replied, coming into the living room.

"They need to be gone within the next twenty-four hours, forty-eight at the latest."

"But dad-"

"But nothing, Freedom. I tried this shit your way and the hole just keeps getting deeper and deeper. I'm not about to watch any of you go to prison or get shot down in the streets, so you're leaving and that's the end of discussion. Black Sam can stay until she helps me locate Sapphire, and then I'll send her behind you. If you want your niggas to go with you, then you better prepare them for immediate evacuation."

"Dad-"

"Freedom, if you open your mouth again, I'ma get up and come over there. It's over, now get out."

Aryanna

# Chapter 16
### Freedom

Two days later...

"You sleep?" he whispered.

"You know I ain't sleep. You know I can't sleep."

"Baby, your dad loves you and he's just worried about you, that's all. From everything you've ever told me about him, how could you expect anything less?"

I knew bone was right, just like I'd known my father was days ago, but that didn't make it any easier to swallow. It wasn't my fault that Destiny had gone on a fucking rampage, yet I knew I was getting blamed and banished for the shit. Despite my father's words to the contrary, and yeah, he'd sent Angel and Destiny to Canada first, but I still felt like I was the one he blamed the most.

I was the one who was supposed to lead in his absence and I'd fallen asleep at the wheel. Now here it was five in the morning and it was my last day on American soil because tomorrow the sun would rise on me in Canada, where I'd rendezvous with my sisters, and it would set on us in Brazil. From there we could go wherever we wanted as long as they wouldn't extradite with the United States. I didn't want to leave, though, not without my father.

"I know he loves me, Bone, but I don't think he understands how much I love him, how much I'd sacrifice for him, even if it meant my life," I said, softly.

"And you think that's what he would want? You think he'd be able to live with himself if he allowed you to make that sacrifice, especially given the fact that you're pregnant? Your father is an intelligent man, Free, so not only does that go against what he knows the right thing is, but he also knows what you've already sacrificed for him. You've been the queen of the streets in a male dominated profession, you and your sisters. Any real nigga is gonna know what it cost you to maintain atop of your empire."

His words rang with truth, almost as if he'd known my father for years, but I knew he understood so well because he was a real nigga himself. I knew Bone loved me, but he also respected me in equal measure. I also knew that part of him was speaking as a father, despite the fact that I was still carrying our child. Thoughts of my unborn little one had me slowly rubbing my stomach as I laid in the bed, watching the shadows slowly disappear as day-light intruded on the night.

I wanted to make all the best decisions for my child and be the type of mother I never had. The problem with that was that the child in my stomach was still an abstract notion, an idea, while my father was a living, breathing person who needed my help. How could I say this to Bone, though, the father of this child, without sounding completely heartless? I loved my child, but if I said anything I was thinking it would come across as the exact opposite.

"It's all gonna work out, babe. You know your dad can handle this situation. Plus, Kamile is a force all her own," he said, snug-gling up closer to me.

"I'm gonna fix something to eat," I said, getting out of bed and going to the kitchen.

After being under the same roof with Angel and Destiny again, it seemed weird for it to be so quiet now. I missed them, but I still didn't wanna go meet up with them. I knew Kamile had my father's back, but her crew was about getting money. Yeah, that required bloodshed at times, but this mission was all about murder.

To make matters worse, the BGF couldn't help with this sit-uation because the indictments were out, which meant mufuckas had to go underground. That left my dad to go up against I don't know how many agents to get his target. Fathergod was more than capable, but anybody could be had, and I would only feel better if I was by his side.

I made myself some sausage and eggs on autopilot, and then sat at the table where I ate it slowly, looking for any type of reasonable argument I could give my dad to change his mind. That would've been hard to do when dealing with an unreasonable man.

"You didn't make me none?" Black Sam asked, coming into the kitchen too wide-eyed to have slept recently.

"I didn't know you were up. You look like you've been up for a while."

"Uh huh," she replied, evasively, fixing herself a bowl of cereal.

"So, what has you up so early?"

"I was facetiming with Destiny as usual. I didn't think I'd miss her this much, and it's not even all about the sex, either. Although, I do miss that."

Listening to her I had no doubt that she probably had been talking to Destiny and she probably did miss her. But watching her as she sat across from me, I saw how fidgety she was. She wasn't telling me the whole truth.

"So, how are my sisters and the fellas?" I asked, resuming the meal in front of me.

"They're good, restless though. They can't wait until you get up there so you all can begin the next leg of your journey.

"You're leaving tonight, right?"

"That's the plan. Are you coming with me?" I asked, still watching her closely.

"Nah, I'll probably be here another day or two, but I'll be watching your backs the whole time."

"Why you staying extra days?"

This question wasn't answered immediately, and her spoon of fruity pebbles damn sure found her mouth with some speed. In this case, not answering was as good as answering.

"What do you know, Samantha?"

"Come on, Free, you know your dad said I'm not to report to anyone except him. You know I love and respect you, but I'm scared of that nigga," she replied truthfully.

I couldn't really blame her, especially since the conversation between her and my father had taken place while he was holding that MAC-12. I could probably put the press on her ass and make her talk, but that wasn't fair. It was an option, though.

"Just tell me this, will all this shit be over soon?" I asked, looking her directly in the eye in order to spot the truth.

"If your father is everything his reputation says he is, then yeah."

I gave her words careful contemplation as I continued eating my food. I knew my father was that nigga, but what her statement really told me was the odds he was going up against. The feds protected their witnesses, especially in RICO cases involving criminal enterprises because the mob had taught them a long time ago that nowhere was too far to go to touch someone. When you added in the fact that my father knew their dirty little secret about my mother being alive while he'd been doing time for her murder, they definitely didn't want him to get to her.

He'd kill her in a loud way that would raise questions. And since he'd already been tried and convicted for her murder, they couldn't charge him again. It was a free homicide, but it could cost him his life. The other thing Black Sam's statement told me was that Sapphire was in town. And if that was the case, then there were only three places she could be.

"Free, don't," Black Sam said.

"Don't what?"

"Come on, Free, you know I know you and I know what you're thinking. Your dad has made his decision, and he's made his feelings clear about defying him. Plus, what happens if you become a liability instead of the help you're intending? You distract him and shit could go wrong for him, or for you. Can you live with that?" she asked sincerely.

I heard the logic in what she was saying, I truly did, but there was no way she could ever convince me that my presence wouldn't help my father.

"So, when are you gonna meet up with Destiny, or are you starting over somewhere else?" I asked, changing the subject.

"I'm gonna catch up with her in Brazil, and then we plan to travel the world for a while."

"That's kinda hard to do when she's a suspect in four capital murder cases," I replied honestly.

"They haven't identified her as the woman in the photos, or Lil Boy either, we're good as long as-"

"They haven't identified her because they're not looking in the right direction. To them, this is just some shit that happens in Chicago on the regular. But once my dad drops Sapphire, you best believe everything and everyone connected to Fathergod will come under scrutiny. Why do you think he made Destiny and Angel leave first? One is wanted, and the other is about to be."

I could tell by the expression on her face that what I'd said had never crossed her mind, but she was damn sure giving it serious thought now. Black Sam ran with us, she was part of the team and a necessity for survival, but she wasn't like us. For her, being a criminal was a choice, but for us, it was about survival so we looked at situations differently. The world wasn't straight, which meant we had to play the angles.

"Well, we'll just stay out of the wrong countries then," she said defensively.

"Calm down, I'm not questioning your relationship, and I damn sure ain't wishing bad on my sister. You can't walk into this blind, though, or both of y'all will get jammed up."

"So, what do you suggest?" she asked.

"Enjoy your time together and live a quiet life as normally as you can. You know Destiny, so you know how much of a challenge that is, but first you have to understand that your old life is over. You may have thought that I didn't want you two together because of mixing business with pleasure, but you see me and Bone conquered the world together. I just knew how much your life would change, especially if you two fell in love."

"I do love her, but it's not a conventional kind of love. Neither of us is gay, so there's gonna be times where dick is involved, but at the end of the day, it's us. We're the foundation. I ain't never felt like that with anyone," she replied, eyes shining brightly with tears.

I knew how she felt because I felt the same way about Bone, minus the other sexual partner aspect. Truthfully, the way I felt about him was what had me reluctant to stay and help my father. Whether it was intentional or not, we had made a family, and that meant something to me. I didn't wanna lose that. I didn't wanna lose my dad either, though. I'd just gotten him back.

"I'm glad you two have each other. Just make sure you understand that once you go to her, there ain't no turning back," I said, getting up and putting my plate in the sink before making my way back to the bedroom.

All that relationship talk made me realize that there was a long overdue conversation that I needed to have. When I went back into the bedroom, Bone was laying down with his eyelids closed, but I knew he wasn't sleep. Picking my phone up off the dresser, I sent a text message, and then I went to get in the shower. Fifteen minutes later, I was dressed in some blue jeans, a white t-shirt, and my navy-blue air force ones.

"Where you going?" Bone asked, sitting up in bed.

"I'm going to see Kamile. There's no telling when I'll see her again after today," I replied, putting my phone in my pocket.

"How you getting there?"

"I told her to send a car for me. It should be in the garage now."

"Hold up, I'm going with you," he said, getting up and searching for something to put on.

"Nah, I wanna do this alone."

"Did I do something wrong?" he asked with a confused look on his face.

"No, baby, I've just got a lot on my mind and I need space to think about it, that's all."

It wasn't in his nature to smother me, but I could see the worry in his eyes was making him want to. If anyone could understand the struggle I was going through, I knew it was him, but some shit I just had to figure out for myself.

"Call if you need me," he said, showing extreme restraint to say or do more.

Crossing to where he was standing, I put my arms around his neck and pulled him down into a passionate kiss that left no room for doubt about how he made me feel.

"Thank you," I whispered against his mouth, letting him go and heading out into the living room.

"Y-you're going out?" Black Sam asked, surprised.

"Calm down. I'm not going to do nothing stupid. I don't even have a gun on me," I replied, not breaking stride and walking out of the apartment.

By the time I took the elevator to the garage, I arrived to find a black 2016 Lincoln Town Car waiting on me, with a driver holding the door open. Once I was in the back seat and on the move, I sent Kamile a text telling her I was on my way. I hadn't planned how this conversation would go, but now that I was in route, I began thinking about my approach. What I had to say was simple, and our friendship should've made it easy to say, but the fact that she was fucking my dad complicated matters.

Within twenty minutes, the car was gliding to a stop in front of her apartment building. I had never been there, but I knew she stayed in one of the penthouse suites so that was my destination as I entered the building and boarded the elevator. The ride up was brief and as soon as the elevator doors opened, the door to the suite directly in front of me opened. The person who opened it wasn't the one I'd expected though.

"It's a little early for you to be out moving around, ain't it?"

"I ain't the one who's wanted, dad. That would be you," I replied, pushing past him into the apartment. The fact that he was there a little after 6am, answering doors wearing nothing but some basketball shorts meant he'd slept there, but that wasn't my business.

As I came further into the apartment I noticed how lavishly Kamile had the place decorated, with paintings on the walls, and art sculptures over stuffed couches and chairs that were a pristine white in color, plush wall to wall white carpeting, and a TV wide enough to be confused with a movie projection screen. If that didn't appeal to you, there was always the view through the panoramic windows. Honestly, it looked like a high-end hotel, but none of those creative comforts could fit in the casket with her, and that's what we needed to discuss.

"Morning, Free," Kamile said, coming into the room wearing only a lavender silk robe.

"Have a seat," she said, sitting on the couch. I took the chair across from her, and my father sat next to her.

"What's on your mind?" she asked.

I could tell by the look on her face that she had an idea what I wanted to talk about, but she hid her unease well, or maybe she thought I wouldn't voice my opinion as harshly with my father sitting there. She was wrong.

"With everything going on I didn't get to address the fact that you're obviously fucking my father," I stated calmly.

"Freedom-"

"It's okay, Johnathan, let her say what she feels," Kamile insisted.

"I'ma do that, anyway, and my father knows that so you ain't gotta be the peacemaker. See, despite his absence, my father knows me very well, and he knows that you and I can have this conversation, or I can kill you," I said, staring at my father the entire time.

I could tell he wanted to say something, but he knew this was between me and Kamile.

"Well… it's obvious you feel some type of way," Kamile replied.

"Feel some type of way? My nigga, if I hadn't known you for as long as I have, and if you hadn't been so helpful recently, I would've let fifty niggas run a train on you before I cut your pussy out with a butcher knife. You know the rules about who you can and can't fuck, and you're in violation."

"I didn't plan for this to-"

"Save the story about how you slipped and fell on his dick because what's done is done. What it comes down to is simple, I'ma leave out of respect for my dad's wishes, but if anything happens or goes sideways, I'ma hunt you and your people first. I promise I'll burn all of Chicago down to get to you, and there's nowhere on planet earth you can run to escape me," I said calmly.

"You don't gotta threaten me, Free, because-"

"I'm not threatening you because a threat means there's a chance that what I'm saying might not happen. I'm guaranteeing it does happen if anything goes wrong."

"When did you start doubting my ability to handle my business?" he asked, clearly offended.

"I never doubt you, dad, but I know it's gonna take more than you, and I don't think her team is up to it. Prove me wrong," I said, standing up.

"Where you going?" he asked.

"To get ready to leave. I said what I had to say, and I'm not gonna argue with you about not going."

He stood up and opened his arms, and I went to him like I always had. The struggle was real when it came to holding my tears back, but I had to because I couldn't do that to him.

"You know I love you with all of my heart, Freedom. And no matter how mad you get, that love will always be the same."

"I love you too, daddy, and I'm not mad at you," I replied squeezing him.

"I will say this, though," I said, backing up so I could look him in the eyes.

"You've got seventy-two hours to put that bitch in the ground and disappear or we're all coming back. It's not up for discussion, so I suggest you spend less time fucking this bitch and more time focusing on what you've risked your life for. It's time to be Fathergod."

# Chapter 17
## Fathergod

"You a'ight?"

"Yeah, I'm good," she replied.

Despite the calm she was trying to put into her voice, I could still detect the stress all over her face. It had been ten minutes since Free left and Kamile had been working to roll the same blunt ever since. I hadn't wasted my time trying to convince her that Free didn't mean what she'd said because we both knew she meant every word. I fully intended to accomplish what I set out to do when it came to Sapphire's treacherous ass, but if I didn't, my child would scorch the earth.

"You don't need to focus on what she said because everything is gonna be fine."

"It's not just what she said, Johnathan. Don't you think I worry about you, too? I know that this is something that has to be done, but I wish you didn't feel the need to handle it personally. Dead is dead, so put a price on that bitch and I'll have a private jet chartered within the hour," she said, looking at me with her heart in her eyes.

When I didn't respond right away, she shook her head sadly and lit her blunt. Kamile was a business woman and that made her ruthless to a certain degree, but she couldn't understand that in some situations you had to pull the trigger yourself. Could I put a price on Sapphire? Yeah. But after all the shit she'd put me and my daughters through, I wanted that bitch's head to come off by my own hands. It wouldn't be right any other way.

"Look, I know you don't understand why I gotta do this myself, but that's the way it is, sweetheart. The concern that you have for me is touching, though, so why don't we focus on what happens when this is all over?"

"What do you mean?" she asked around a mouth full of smoke.

"I mean, are you coming with me?"

Now it was her turn to hesitate before answering, but I already knew the truth about what was happening between us. Kamile had always known how Free would react to her and I, which was why she'd moved with extreme caution. The fact that it had still gone down, though, said a lot about how she felt because she was too intelligent and calculating to risk her life over some dick, even good dick.

"You know you fucked up about me, so why sit there and bullshit like you don't know what you want?"

"And what is it you think I want?" she asked, passing me the blunt.

My left hand guided the blunt to my mouth while my right reached into my shorts and pulled my dick out. She tried hard to keep her eyes off it, but the way the corner of her mouth was twitching I could tell she wanted to smile.

"That's all you think I want, huh?" she asked, taking it from my hand and stroking it gently.

When her robe fell, open I got a look at her gorgeous body right before she made her move to get on top of me, and take me inside her.

"This is what it's all about for you? You want this good pussy, don't you, Fathergod?"

Hearing her use my street name made me put the blunt in the ashtray next to the couch and put my hands on her hips to stop her from moving.

"What's wrong?" I asked, searching her face intently.

"Nothing's wrong, except you're stopping the flow of what we were doing?"

"Don't lie to me, Kamile. I know something's wrong because you called me Fathergod."

"That's who you are, ain't you? That's who the world expects you to be, including your children. So why shouldn't I call you that?"

"Because that's not what I am with you," I replied softly. Taking her face in my hands and watching as her tears built up quicker than a summer's storm.

I'd loved once, and that love had been my gift and my curse so I'd never had much use for the emotion outside of the relationship I had with my daughters. For the first time in a long time, I thought I could love again, and it was this woman who made me feel this forbidden feeling. Pulling her face to mine, I kissed her gently, yet thoroughly, tasting both the salt of her tears and the pineapple Kush on her breath. Despite the fact that she was on top of me and I was inside her, my kiss was still asking for something.

As my tongue danced with hers, I sought forgiveness and understanding, and when she finally started to ride me slowly, I felt like I had my answers. For endless minutes, her speed didn't increase, but our kiss deepened as we communicated in the simplest way about all that couldn't be said. It didn't matter how many times we'd been there before, the sensations that rocked my body when I was inside her were always new and amazing.

"Say my name," I whispered against her mouth.

"Jon-Johnathan," she rasped.

"I want you to say it like you mean it," I demanded, grabbing her by the hips and pushing up into her with deliberate and hard strokes.

"Johnathan!"

Wrapping my arms around her I stood up and carried her to the bedroom, where I made love to her with unrestrained passion for the next hour. I didn't wanna stop and I didn't wanna leave, but it was time to get back to business.

"You never answered my question," I said, while I was getting dressed.

"And what question was that?"

"Are you coming with me?" I asked again.

"I thought I did answer that, you didn't feel this pussy rain on you once you came inside me?"

My response to her question was to look at her so she would quit bullshittin' because I was serious.

"Damn, you can't take a joke, Johnathan?"

"This ain't the time for that. I need to know what's up because this shit with Sapphire could pop off any day. And once it's done, I'm gone."

"Well, considering the fact that I've been letting you cum in me with no condom, and before you ask, no, I'm not on birth control, it's evident on my part that I'm trying to start a new life with you. I'ma go wherever that takes us, even if it's straight to hell," she replied, smiling at me from her reclined position on the bed.

Leaning down, I gave her a kiss meant to make her heart beat out of her chest.

"No matter where we go, as long as we do it together, then that's all that matters. I got you," I told her, kissing her again quickly before I finished putting my shirt on and buttoning it.

"Call downstairs and get the car for me. Are you available for me to cook you a little dinner tonight, or are you working?" I asked.

"I'm always working, but if my man demands my time, then that's just what it is. What time should I be at your place, or are you coming here to cook?"

"I'll meet you here at about 7pm. That good for you?"

"Yeah, but take the key card by the door in case you get here early," she replied. "Guess I'll see you later then."

For a moment, our eyes locked and we communicated without words. I love that we could speak this language because I wasn't one of them R&B type niggas, but I did feel shawty on a whole different level than anyone I'd known. I might not have been able to say it, but I could show it.

"I'll see you later, sweetheart," I said, smiling.

"Be safe, babe."

As hard as it was, I walked out the room, but in my mind, I still saw her in the many positions we'd been in a short while ago. I made sure to grab the key card and put it in my pocket on my way out to the elevator. When I got downstairs to the garage, Kamile's personally chauffeured Escalade was waiting on me. And once I hopped in, we pulled off.

Traffic was a little hectic with people trying to get to work, but my mind was more focused on what my next move was for the day. I had a feeling that something might be going on because for Free to put me on a seventy-two-hour clock, she had to know something that she shouldn't. I knew Black Sam was her friend and a loyal employee, and originally, I wouldn't interfere with that, but Free didn't know how to get out of her own way, so I had to tell Black Sam to keep her out of the business.

Based on Free's statement, I was now wondering if my orders had been obeyed. It took thirty minutes to get back to my apartment building, but instead of going to my apartment, I went to the one Free was still occupying. For a full two minutes, my knocks went unanswered, and then Black Sam opened the door.

"Where's my daughter?" I asked, moving past her into the apartment.

"H-her and Bone had some last-minute things to do before they left tonight."

"Close the door and come here," I demanded.

The hesitation in her every move was indicative of the fear she felt, but she knew that disobeying me wasn't an option, so she did as told and came to stand in front of me.

"Free came to see Kamile this morning, and I just happened to be there. After she said what she'd come to say, she informed me that I had seventy-two hours to wrap this shit up or she'd bring everybody back to do it. I didn't think anything of it at the time, but in order for her to give me such a short timeframe, she'd have to be damn certain that I could get to Sapphire... and the only one who could tell her that would be you," I said, looking at her closely, knowing what would happen if she was dishonest in this moment.

"I-I didn't tell her where Sapphire is. I sw-swear," she insisted, trembling slightly.

"So, what exactly did you tell her?'

"Sh-she asked if this would all be over s-soon, and I said it would if you were everything your reputation said you were," she replied, fighting the tears that were now clouding her vision.

Just based on what she said, I knew what Free had heard. What surprised me was that Free hadn't tried to make a move on her own, which hopefully meant she was learning from the last mistake she made like that. That was something I would congratulate her on later. Right now, I needed the facts about my soon to be dead wife.

"What did you find out about Sapphire?" I asked.

"The FBI rented two adjoining rooms at the Sheraton Hotel and she's set to be at the federal courthouse in the morning."

"Two rooms? How many agents are guarding her?"

"From what I can tell, it's only the two in the room next to hers, but there could be more doing a walking patrol throughout the hotel," she replied.

"That doesn't add up. I mean, I would've thought they'd have her under the protection and watch of the national guard, given the testimony she's about to give, and given the fact that I'm on the loose."

"I think the last place the FBI would ever expect you to be is Chicago, and so many bodies have already been snatched due to the indictments that there's probably nobody left to put in the work. The soldiers and enforcers are in jail, and the big homies are on the run."

What she said was true, and I knew that part because I'd gotten word from Tony Mack that Sapphire had known enough to blow a hole in the organization. Of course, once he revealed that, he'd had to die because most of it was his fault. Tender dick niggas who engaged in pillow talk couldn't be trusted.

"How do I get to her?" I asked, keeping my focus on what need to be done next.

"Let me get my laptop," she said, dashing off into the back of the apartment.

I wanted to move with as much stealth as possible. But if push came to shove, I'd level the whole goddamn building and be done with it. From the moment, the homies had gotten wind that there was a rat within the organization, and the investigation turned up a female with a history in my part of the world, I'd had an indescribable feeling. I don't know how I knew it was Sapphire, but I didn't believe in coincidence.

The deeper my people dug into Sapphire's death, the less shit made sense because how her nigga's body was recovered, but hers was burned beyond recognition never rang true. I'd left both of them in the same place, downstairs in the living room. I know one anomaly would lead to another, but the FBI got wind of my investigation and that's when they snatched me and put me in a prison under a different identity.

That right there was verification that I was on to something, and now I was getting ready to face the woman who ruined my life. I could damn near taste her death on my tongue, and it was sweeter than anybody else I'd killed.

"Okay, so the Sheraton has more of a business clientele," Black Sam began, coming back into the living room and sitting on the couch so she could put her laptop on the coffee table.

"I figure if you walk in with a suit on and a briefcase, you're gonna look just like any other out of town businessman. Keep it simple. It would help, though, if Kamile could have some chicks already in the building as maids, maybe even someone on room service, so you can verify that she's in the room and she's alone. I can create positions in the hotel database that go back at least a year, and I'll be controlling all the cameras so I can erase y'all's presence. Do you wanna kill her on the spot, or kidnap her?" she asked seriously.

As badly as I wanted to take my time with this bitch, I felt to do that would be spitting in the face of the good fortune that was smiling on me at the moment. I needed to just make this quick and painless, and move on.

"I'ma drop her where she stands," I replied.

"A'ight, well, if you're gonna use a gun then make sure you got a silencer on it so the neighbors don't hear it. I assume you're doing this ASAP, right?"

"As soon as I'm done with you, I'm going to call Kamile and put everything into play for tonight after Free is gone. I don't want her getting any wild ideas," I said, knowing how hard headed my daughter was. I'd get this shit done and be out of town right behind her.

"Okay, well I'ma make the necessary arrangements for us to vanish in the middle of the night."

"Make sure you make arrangements for Kamile, too, because she's coming with me," I said, loving how that sounded coming out of my mouth.

"Oh, um, okay. I'll get on top of everything now and you handle what you gotta handle."

"Samantha, don't say shit to Free about this. Matter of fact, get all your shit and come to my apartment because I'd hate to have to kill you first."

I made that statement as an off-handed joke, but we both knew I was serious. It was go time and I didn't need any distractions.

# Aryanna

# Chapter 18
# Fathergod

I kept Black Sam held up in the apartment until we had everything straight down to the key card for my hotel room on the same floor as Sapphire. Kamile already had her girls infiltrating the hotel, which was easy because she provided entertainment for many parties, and the manager was a fan of the 'extra' treatment her employees offered. We had eyes on Sapphire, and I didn't have to go in carrying any guns because what I needed would be waiting on me in the room. That didn't mean I was leaving home without my Glock .45 because if I was noticed by anyone, I wanted to be ready to hold court.

As the day wore on and all the details were taken care of by other people, I let Black Sam go back next door long enough to make sure Free and Bone were set to travel. They had a long drive ahead of them to get to Vermont, where they could then cross into Canada. But at the moment, I just wanted them outside the city limits before shit got real.

Everybody, including me and Black Sam, had new paperwork and passports, so all that was left for Free and Bone to do was hop in the Range Rover Kamile had given them and put Chicago in the rearview. We'd already said our goodbyes so I wasn't expecting them to come to my apartment. But when Black Sam came back, I knew they were gone. Now my complete and undivided attention was on my showdown with Sapphire, and it was long overdue.

"You look good in that suit. You should blend in nicely," Sam commented.

"Of course, I look good, it's Black Billionaire tailor made, but I don't know about me blending in. I'm a big nigga."

"True shit. That's why you're not coming in through the front door, but through the garage instead, like you've already checked into your room. Once you get to the hotel, you make the call and Kamile's girl is gonna bring you the key card to run the elevator. Your room is on the 10th floor, number 1017 to be exact, and it's at the end of the hallway. Sapphire is right around the corner in 1023. But since the elevator opens up on your side of the hallway, the two feds sitting outside her door won't see you."

"So, is it two outside her door and two in the room next door?" I asked.

"Yeah, plus two downstairs that do perimeter checks every fifteen minutes."

"What about inside her room? Is she alone?"

"We ain't been able to get nobody in because the feds is running interference, so what's behind that door is a mystery," she replied truthfully.

"I'll handle whatever comes to get that bitch."

"I figured you felt that way so my suggestion is you knock off the four feds first. When Kamile's girl meets you in the garage, she's also gonna give you a master key card that'll get you into both rooms. All of this should take no more than fifteen minutes, and I'll be watching," she said, tapping the laptop in her hand reassuringly.

"And when it's over?"

"You'll go out the same way you came in, and meet me and Kamile in Detroit. The driver already knows to drive non-stop. The route's been picked, and there will be some hardware on board in case shit goes sideways. The jet is chartered and waiting on us."

"I don't want you to leave until I'm out of that building," I said.

"What, why?" she asked, her face contoured by confusion,

"Because anything could go wrong, and I want you on deck, not on the road, in case we have to improvise. I'll come here to get you. The hotel is only ten minutes away from here."

I could see the unease on her face, but she had to know that she was in it now and we were gonna play this by my rules.

"Are we clear?" I asked, just to ensure that there was no confusion.

"We're clear."

I felt my phone vibrate in my pocket, so I pulled it out to check my text messages.

"The car is upstairs, which means there ain't no time for bullshittin'."

"What about your stuff?" she asked.

"There's nothing I got that can't be replaced. Plus, both apartments will be swept and cleaned out once we're gone. We're ghosts now, nothing more than memories that'll one day fade away. I hope you're prepared for that because it's no turning back."

# Aryanna

# Chapter 19
## Freedom

"You okay, babe?"

"Yeah, I'm fine," I replied softly, looking out the window, but not really seeing the passing landscape that was fading into the shadows of evening.

"You ain't really said shit since we left."

"What am I supposed to say, Bone? You want me to tell you how wrong this feels, how much I feel like I'm deserting my own father because I'm scared?"

"No one thinks you're scared, Free. It ain't about being scared. It's about being smart and staying out of harm's way," he replied.

"But I don't live my life that way, Bone. I'm front line for mine, and you know this," I said, frustrated.

"I understand, but you can't be that right now. You gotta think about the baby-"

"I can have another baby, but I only got one goddamn father," I yelled, angry at myself for the tears I could feel in my eyes.

We rode along in silence for a few moments and I thought it was because Bone just didn't wanna argue, but then I realized what I'd said.

"Bone, I didn't-I didn't mean it like that," I said softly, checking my anger.

"How else could you mean it, Freedom? It's obvious our baby doesn't matter as much to you as your dad does, so why didn't you just have an abortion?"

"That's not fair," I replied, getting angry all over again.

His response was to turn and look at me, and then he went right back to navigating the highway. In truth, my anger wasn't at him for what he'd said, but at myself because thoughts of abortion and miscarriage had previously crossed my mind. I was mad at myself for being selfish.

I loved the baby growing inside of me… at least I wanted to. I just didn't know how to spread my love around between the people I cared about out here in the world with me, and the little one inside me. It seemed like someone was always coming up short.

"Bone, I love you and I know that you know that by now. I love this child because you and I created it, and I wouldn't do that with anyone in the world other than you. But he's my father, Bone, my father, and I feel like I'm leaving him for dead."

I knew he was hearing me, but he didn't respond or acknowledge my words in any way. It was obvious I'd hurt him, and that was truly the last thing I ever wanted to do because he was a major part of everything I was. We were seated side by side, no more than a few inches apart, but it felt like we were on opposite ends of the universe.

I hadn't meant to give words to my innermost feelings, and now that I had there was no way to take it back or smooth it over. All I could do was shut up so I didn't say shit else stupid, and that's exactly what I did, looking out the window at scenery that was no more interesting than it had been ten minutes ago.

I needed to focus on shaking this negative feeling I was having like I had to be at my father's side, like he couldn't handle his own wax. His reputation, his nickname, and the fear that came with it were all things that he earned without me holding his hand, so it was arrogant of me to think I had to do that now.

He'd forgotten more about the streets and bodying shit than I'd ever learn, and I needed to remember that instead of insulting his gangsta. Even as I was telling myself all that, I still couldn't shake the feeling like I was leaving my heart in Chicago. There was nothing I could do about it now, though.

"I love you," I said, reaching out and taking his free hand in mine, lacing our fingers together.

The fact that he didn't pull away was encouraging, even though he didn't say the words back. I knew he loved me, though.

"Bone what-what are you doing?" I asked, when he pulled an abrupt U-turn and pointed the truck in the direction we'd just come from.

"I'm loving you."

"But what about the baby, I-"

"I didn't say we were going to hop on the front line, but we can be close by whenever shit jumps off just in case we're needed," he said, squeezing my hand reassuringly.

I didn't have the words to express how I was feeling right now, but my heart was beating so hard in my chest that I knew he had to feel the vibrations in my fingertips.

I pulled his hand up to my lips and kissed it, needing to do something to display my love and gratitude for the man sitting beside me who was putting my feelings over his own. That was shit only real niggas did for their women.

"My dad's gonna be pissed," I said, cringing slightly at the verbal ass whooping I was gonna take.

"Good thing I ain't scared of him then, huh?"

All I could do was smile because I knew he was telling the truth. We were already an hour and a half outside of the city, but we made the drive back in 45 minutes. Both of us knew there was a risk to speeding because we were both packing pistols, and my new AR-15 was on the floorboard at my feet. Yeah, it was dumb to move like that, but fuck it.

"I'm not even gonna put the ass chewing off, I'm just gonna go tell him we're staying and he has to deal with it," I said, once we reached the building and we were riding down in the elevator.

"Youi want me to go with you?"

"Nah, I can handle him. Wait for me at the apartment. The key is over top of the door frame."

Going to my father's apartment, I took a deep breath and knocked. After waiting what I thought was a reasonable amount of time, I knocked again, hoping he wasn't back out with Kamile because I really wanted to talk to him. I was just about to assume the worse when I heard movement from the other side of the door.

"Dad, I can hear you moving. Open the door so we can talk," I said, knocking again.

"Dad?" I called.

I raised my hand to start hammering on the door when it was suddenly pulled open and I came face to face with Black Sam.

"Bitch, I know you heard me. What took you so long?" I asked, pushing past her into the apartment.

"I was doing something on the computer, but what the hell are you doing here, Free?"

I spun around intending to ask her who the fuck she was talking to, but the fear on her face stopped me. Since I knew I hadn't said or done anything to inspire that fear, it could only mean one thing.

"Where is he?" I asked.

"Who? I don't know-"

Pulling the .38 revolver from the waist band of my jeans froze her lies in mid-air quickly.

"Samantha, where the fuck is my father?" I asked slowly.

"Y-you should sit down, there's a lot to explain."

# Chapter 20
## Fathergod

If you ever had the chance, or misfortunate, of running into a real killer, you'd know that he or she was as calm as a sleeping baby. You never saw nerves or fear, just the clear calculation in their eyes as they assessed the situation and ran different scenarios of how shit could play out. That was how things appeared on the outside, but inside, their heart was always beating fast. It wouldn't show in the hands or any other outward signs because by the time they reached the status of an actual killer, they would've mastered the act of masking weakness. But the adrenaline still flowed, and their heart knocked in their chest harder than any bass.

I knew that because I was a killer, and even as I stood stone still riding the elevator to the long overdue rendezvous, I could feel my heart beat in my jawline. Had there been anyone else on the elevator, I would've appeared to be nothing more than a well-dressed businessman with normal privileges and issues, but inside my body was alive in a way that only happened right before the curtain went up and the show began. The elevator came to a smooth stop, the doors slid open, and I felt the calm before the storm wash over me as I stepped off and moved to the right, where my room was.

Based on the layout that Kamile's employees sent to my phone, I knew Sapphire's room was to the left and around the corner, but it wasn't time to make my move yet. With purposeful strides, I made it to my door and let myself inside the room. Once I had the door locked, I moved straight to the bed and searched beneath it for the briefcase I knew I would find. Laying it out on the bed, I opened it to find twin black Glock 9mm's with silencers already screwed on the ends, and extra clips.

After checking both clips in the guns to make sure they were fully loaded, I put the extras in my pocket, and took my phone out to text Black Sam that I was ready. On her cue, she was gonna have one of Kamile's girls come down the hallway from the opposite end, which would draw the agent's attention away from me bending the corner behind them. It was hard to believe the day of reckoning was there, but I was damn sure ready for it. It was the longest three minutes of my life before I got the text back from Black Sam saying it was show time. But once I did, I grabbed the pistols and headed for the door.

Once I was in the hallway, there wasn't an ounce of hesitation in my steps when I turned the corner with both guns levelled out in front of me. Both FBI agents were in conversation with the slender brown skin maid, and because of that, their backs were to me. The agent closest to me had his brain matter scattered all over his partner's navy blue suit with two coughs from the barrel of the pistol jumping in my hand, and when his partner turned to face me, he was looking at death.

"Don't breathe, don't reach, or you get what he did. Baby girl, relieve him of the pistol beneath his right arm and then disappear," I instructed calmly.

Both parties did as they were told as I closed the distance between us. Once the girl vanished around the corner, I decided to get on with the show.

"Turn around and let yourself into room 1024, nice and slow like because my trigger finger got a mind of its own," I said, jamming both guns into his back.

I kept a close eye on him while he reached in his pocket for the key card, knowing he was probably expecting me to be distracted by trying to watch my surroundings, but I had eyes in the sky. As soon as he pushed the door open, I pulled both triggers, and stepped over his body while taking aim at the two agents sitting at the table by the window, playing cards.

"What the-" was all either man got to say before a steady diet of bullets ended their lives.

Tucking one pistol behind my back alongside my other Glock, I backed up into the hallway while pulling out the master key card. Thirty seconds later, I was strolling into Sapphire's room, where I found her sitting on her bed with a tablet in her lap. The woman before me looked nothing like the one I remembered, except for the shape of her body. I didn't know how bad her burns had been, but her beauty was flawless by any standard. Still, all I could see was the ugliness of everything she stood for.

"Long time no see Sapphire, or should I call you Jewel?" I asked, gripping my pistol tighter.

"Y-you've got me confused with someone else."

There was only a little hitch in her voice, but the look in her eyes said it all in one word. Terrified. Every day I'd spent in prison, every moment I was away from my daughters, it was all worth it because I got to see this look in her eyes.

"I've got you confused? Well maybe I should just apologize and leave… or maybe I should rip the bottom half of your jaw off and have my people run your dental records. If I'm wrong I can admit it after the fact," I said, smiling, advancing on her slowly.

"Please I-"

"Wait, I know you ain't about to beg for your life. I know you not gonna do that after all the shit you've done. You gotta know that at the very least you deserve to die," I said reasonably.

"Jon-Johnathan, my son, I've got-"

"Yeah, I know, you gotta son. You've also got three daughters, or did you forget about them? You know, I thought when this moment came, I'd wanna know why you did what you did, but honestly it really doesn't matter. All that matters is that you die," I said, raising the pistol and pointing it at her pretty face.

"Mom-mom what's going on? Why are you crying?"

Through our whole exchange, I'd never noticed that she'd been facetiming, mainly because she'd turned the tablet to where I couldn't see the screen. But I guess in reality of her fate, she'd wanted to say goodbye to the face on the screen. As Fathergod, I did grant last requests in most cases, but the face on the screen had me too paralyzed to even tell her that.

"I thought your son… wait, turn that so I can see it fully," I demanded, stepping to the foot of the bed.

She did like I told her and the longer I stared at her little boy the more disbelief set in. I knew that face. In fact, it was my face when I was his age.

"His father…" I said weakly. "His father isn't-"

Before I could get the words out, the force of a sledge hammer hit me in the chest and lifted me off my feet. The gun in my hand disappeared better than any magic trick I'd ever seen, and even though my mind was screaming for me to reach for one of the other pistols I had on me, I couldn't get my body to cooperate. The taste of copper in my mouth told me that the bullet inside me had hit something of importance, and the sight of Sapphire advancing on me with a .357 outstretched in her hand told me more bullets would follow. For a minute, she just stood over me staring with eyes void of emotion and expression. Even with the knowledge we both shared, I knew I was nothing to her, but the feeling was mutual.

"He's your son, Johnathan," she whispered. "But he won't miss you and neither will I."

There was nothing I could say to change the circumstances, but my last thought wasn't of the son I didn't know, it was of the daughters I was leaving behind. I knew they'd avenge me out of love. I just wished I'd done things differently.

# Chapter 21
### Freedom

"Bone, we have to go."

"Free, it's already in motion. Samantha just told you that he's already inside the hotel."

"I know where he is and we're going to him, now," I said, heading for the front door.

"Black Sam, contact Kamile's girl and tell her to meet us in the garage so we can get into the building," Bone said, following me out the door and into the elevator.

It had taken everything in me not to blow Samantha's head clean the fuck off because that bitch should've told me this shit was gonna go down tonight. Luckily for her, she was still useful to me or she'd be another body for the Chicago coroner to pick up.

"Slow ass elevator," I growled, wishing I had taken the stairs instead.

"Baby, calm down. Your dad can handle his own."

"I know that, but he's going into this situation by his god-damn self because them rookie bitches Kamile hired ain't bout nothing. This is the FBI we are talking 'bout, Bone, and it's at least six of them, if not more," I said, becoming more and more angry at myself for leaving in the first place.

"Black Sam said it's six total, and you know how good she is at what she does."

"Yeah, well, she better hope she's good. Give me the keys," I demanded, once the elevator doors opened into the garage.

With them in my hand, I was damn near running to get to the truck.

"Let me get in first, shit," Bone exclaimed as I got behind the wheel, cranked the engine, and put the truck in gear before he even had his door open.

If he didn't understand that I was in a hurry, then his ass was about to get left behind for real. No sooner than his ass hit the leather seat, I had the truck sideways to avoid smashing into someone, but once I was pointed in the direction of the hotel, I stood on the gas pedal with all my might.

"Baby, can you at least try to get us there in one piece? I mean, damn, you're all over the road."

"Shut up and make sure my AR-15 is locked and loaded, and get the extra clips out of the glove compartment," I ordered, swerving in and out of traffic, narrowly avoiding hitting several cars.

The hotel was only ten minutes from the apartment building, according to Black Sam's directions, but I had us fishtailing into the underground garage in six minutes flat.

"Where the fuck is this bitch?" I asked, frustrated that she wasn't in front of the elevators when I slid the truck to a stop.

"I'll call Sam and-"

"There she is," I said, hopping out of the truck and going to where she stood holding the elevator door open.

"Where is he?"

"He's on the 10th floor," she replied, handing me a standard issue Glock .40.

Once we were on the elevator, I popped the clip out of the gun to make sure it was loaded, slammed it back in, and pushed a bullet into the chamber. The sound of Bone doing the same thing with the AR-15 was comforting, but the slow ass elevator had me ready to hop out of my skin.

"I think he's got everything under control," the girl in the maid uniform said, looking at me through the reflection of the elevator doors.

"Bitch, did I ask you what the fuck you thought?" I asked, jamming the pistol into the back of her head hard enough to make her head-butt the elevator door.

"Free, don't" Bone said.

I wasn't trying to hear what he was saying either, but the only reason I didn't pull the trigger was because I didn't wanna alert any FBI agents lurking around. And lucky for her, we'd arrived on the 10th floor.

"Which way?" I asked the frightened girl.

"A-around the corner."

We already knew the room number, and when we bent the corner we did so with guns up and ready. I was scanning the hotel rooms on both sides of the hallway looking for 1023, but when I spotted the bodies of the FBI agents and the two open hotel room doors, I knew we arrived.

"Keep your eyes open," I said, creeping up on the first open door.

I don't know what I'd expected to find when I rounded that corner into the room, but what I saw brought me to my knees instantly. I wanted to deny it, or blink it away, or unsee it, but none of those options was possible. A few feet from me lay the man that I loved more than anything in the world, the carpet around him stained crimson with his blood.

"Da-daddy," I whispered, crawling towards him slowly.

"No, daddy, please," I whined, dropping the pistol and taking his head into my lap.

My heart stopped when his eyes suddenly flickered open and focused on my face.

"Fr-Freedom, what are you doing here?" he asked, just above a whisper.

"I came back, daddy. I couldn't leave you alone. I love you too much," I said, fighting a losing battle against the sob in my throat as my tears rained on him with the weight of a thousand bricks.

"I l-love you t-too, baby. I'm sorry."

"It's okay, you don't have to apologize. Save your strength. Bone, call 911," I screamed, trying not to panic.

"No time, Free, l-listen to me," my dad said, struggling to breathe.

At that point, all I could do was listen because I was crying too hard to talk. The guilt I felt in that moment was only matched by my sadness and my stupidity. I'd made the ultimate mistake and gone against my instincts, and it might've cost me more than I could ever afford to pay.

"S-Sapphire-Sapphire's son, you gotta protect him-"

"Did Sapphire do this?" I asked, feeling pure rage threaten to consume me at just that thought alone.

"Y-yes, but her s-son. Protect him F-Free. Please. Get him from h-her," my dad said, coughing up blood in a way that frightened me and rocked me to my foundation.

"Daddy, please stop talking," I begged, sobbing openly now.

He looked up at me and gave me one of his rare smiles that transformed his entire face.

"I love y-you, Freedom Walker. I always w-will. Protect him, he's your b-brother… he's my son."

The shock of what my father just said was as powerful as finding him laid on the floor shot, but I didn't have time to feel it.

"Daddy! Daddy, please, please don't leave me again. Daddy, don't go," I screamed.

He was still smiling at me, but the light in his eyes had gone dark. The unthinkable had happened. My daddy was dead…

To Be Continued…
The Boss Man's Daughter's 3:
Queens of Destruction

# Stay Connected with Us!

Text **LOCKDOWN** to 22828 to stay up-to-date with new releases, sneak peaks, contests and more…

Thank you!

## Coming Soon from Lock Down Publications/Ca$h Presents

BOW DOWN TO MY GANGSTA

By **Ca$h & Jamaica**

TORN BETWEEN TWO

By **Coffee**

CUM FOR ME **III**

By **Ca$h & Company**

BLOOD OF A BOSS **IV**

By **Askari**

BRIDE OF A HUSTLA **III**

By **Destiny Skai**

WHEN A GOOD GIRL GOES BAD **II**

By **Adrienne**

LOVE & CHASIN' PAPER **II**

By **Qay Crockett**

THE HEART OF A GANGSTA **II**

By **Jerry Jackson**

TO DIE IN VAIN **II**

By **ASAD**

THE BOSS MAN'S DAUGHTERS **III**

By **Aryanna**

UNBREAK MY HEART

By **Misty Holt**

A DOPEBOY'S PRAYER **II**

By **Eddie "Wolf" Lee**

**Available Now**

**(CLICK TO PURCHASE)**

RESTRAING ORDER **I & II**

By **CA$H & Coffee**

LOVE KNOWS NO BOUNDARIES **I II & III**

By **Coffee**

LAY IT DOWN **I & II**

LAST OF A DYING BREED

By **Jamaica**

PUSH IT TO THE LIMIT

By **Bre' Hayes**

BLOOD OF A BOSS **I II & III**

By **Askari**

THE STREETS BLEED MURDER **I, II & III**

THE HEART OF A GANGSTA

By **Jerry Jackson**

CUM FOR ME

CUM FOR ME 2

An **LDP Erotica Collaboration**

BRIDE OF A HUSTLA **I & II**

By **Destiny Skai**

WHEN A GOOD GIRL GOES BAD

By **Adrienne**

A GANGSTER'S REVENGE **I II III & IV**

THE BOSS MAN'S DAUGHTERS

A SAVAGE LOVE **I & II**

By **Aryanna**

A DOPEBOY'S PRAYER

By **Eddie "Wolf" Lee**

WHAT ABOUT US **I & II**

NEVER LOVE AGAIN

THUG ADDICTION

By **Kim Kaye**

THE KING CARTEL **I, II & III**

By **Frank Gresham**

THESE NIGGAS AIN'T LOYAL **I, II & III**

By **Nikki Tee**

GANGSTA SHYT **I II &III**

By **CATO**

THE ULTIMATE BETRAYAL

By **Phoenix**

DON'T FU#K WITH MY HEART **I & II**

By **Linnea**

BOSS'N UP **I & II**

By **Royal Nicole**

I LOVE YOU TO DEATH

**By Destiny J**

I RIDE FOR MY HITTA

I STILL RIDE FOR MY HITTA

By **Misty Holt**

LOVE & CHASIN' PAPER

By **Qay Crockett**

TO DIE IN VAIN

By **ASAD**

## BOOKS BY LDP'S CEO, CA$H
### (CLICK TO PURCHASE)

TRUST IN NO MAN

TRUST IN NO MAN 2

TRUST IN NO MAN 3

BONDED BY BLOOD

SHORTY GOT A THUG

THUGS CRY

THUGS CRY 2

TRUST NO BITCH

TRUST NO BITCH 2

TRUST NO BITCH 3

TIL MY CASKET DROPS

RESTRAINING ORDER

RESTRAINING ORDER 2

IN LOVE WITH A CONVICT

### Coming Soon

THUGS CRY 3

BONDED BY BLOOD 2

BOW DOWN TO MY GANGSTA

www.ingramcontent.com/pod-product-compliance
Lightning Source LLC
Chambersburg PA
CBHW070026260626
47159CB00005B/1966